M

BEST SELLER ROMANCE

A chance to read and collect some of the best-loved novels from Mills & Boon—the world's largest publisher of romantic fiction.

Every month, four titles by favourite Mills & Boon authors will be re-published in the *Best Seller Romance* series.

A list of other titles in the *Best Seller Romance* series can be found at the end of this book.

Charlotte Lamb

FORBIDDEN FIRE

MILLS & BOON LIMITED
15–16 BROOK'S MEWS
LONDON W1A 1DR

*First published in Great Britain 1979
by Mills & Boon Limited*

© Charlotte Lamb 1979

*Australian copyright 1979
Philippine copyright 1979
This edition 1984*

ISBN 0 263 74981 9

*Set in Linotype Times 11 on 12 pt.
02–1284*

*Made and printed in Great Britain by
Richard Clay (The Chaucer Press) Ltd,
Bungay, Suffolk*

CHAPTER ONE

THE June sky was a deep, halcyon blue above rolling green pastures lustred with buttercups, as the slow, stopping train from Bristol drew into a station banked with cottage garden flowers; stocks, pinks, larkspur, their warm colours and summer fragrance giving the bare little platform the air of a tiny oasis. Louise had been leaning against the window, tracing the familiar view mile by mile, eagerness sparking in her enormous blue eyes, unaware of the glances of the other passengers who could not help smiling at the slender, black-haired schoolgirl whose straw hat shadowed a small, oval face of startling, delicate beauty.

As the train drew to a stop she leapt down, turning to retrieve her case. The smile she gave to the man who handed it down to her was dazzling, and he blinked before smiling back.

She put down the case, turning to stare along the empty platform. The guard blew his whistle. The door slammed shut behind her. The train began to draw out of the station and she was left alone, breathing in the warm perfume of the flowers, hearing the slow silence of the summer afternoon return. There were swallows nesting in the station eaves. Their darting flight crossed the lines, a melodic note in their voices. Louise sighed pleasurably, waiting without alarm. He would come, she never doubted that. Her blue eyes saw him suddenly, turning in through the gate, and she flew to meet him, light as a feather as she raced into his arms.

'Daniel!' Her smooth cheek pressed against his face, she threw her arms around his neck, and felt his arms come round her slowly to enclose her.

Ever since she was eight years old there had been the same homecoming. Daniel would hold out his arms and she would race into them, her body as slight as a wand, her long black hair wayward, eager to feel the possessive strength of his arms holding her.

She let herself yield entirely, waiting for him to swing her round in a wide circle, as he always did, her feet off the ground, her laughter spilling around them both.

It was then that she sensed a difference in the long-established ritual of her first day home. Instead of lifting her off her feet and swinging her round, Daniel carefully released her, pushing her very gently away from him.

She raised puzzled, startled eyes to his hard, brown face, a suddenly serious expression coming into the oval features.

'Welcome home, Louise,' he said levelly. 'Did you have a good journey? The car is outside. I'll get your case.'

He strode away, a tall, lean man in elegantly casual summer clothes, the silver threads in his dark hair glinting in the sunlight, his blue shirt rippling across his wide shoulders as a faint breeze caught it. She stared after him, wondering what was wrong, knowing with childlike, disappointed bewilderment that since they last met there had been some indefinable alteration in their relationship. Until today she had always known what he was thinking, feeling, as if their minds were secretly linked, invisibly telepathic.

It hurt her deeply to sense a barrier where there had been none before. For some reason Daniel had excluded her, and Louise watched him intently, wondering why.

He turned and came back carrying her case; his eyes, neither green nor blue but somewhere in between, brilliantly opalescent in the sunlight, not quite meeting her glance. She followed silently as he strode out of the station. The stationmaster appeared at the barrier, grinning at her in recognition, taking her proffered ticket.

'Home for the holidays, Louise? You'll be glad to see Queen's Dower again?'

Her smile shone out briefly, the blue eyes friendly. 'Yes,' she said, aware of understatement. 'How are you, Mr Fife? Are the boys well?'

'They're just fine,' he said. 'Like you, they're growing up ... you look older every time I see you.'

'Give them my love,' she said lightly, passing on out of the station.

Daniel had reached the car, was stowing her case in the wide boot of the long white car. She saw him straighten, slamming the boot as if he needed to perform some act of violence. He glanced towards her, his hand pushing back a ruffled windblown lock of silver-threaded dark hair. As she quickly walked towards him her eyes caught the figure seated in the front passenger seat and a coolness came into her face. Daniel stood, the back door held open, and she slid into the seat, removing her straw hat.

The woman turned, her dark eyes faintly hostile. 'Hallo, Louise,' she said. 'Have a good journey?'

'Yes, thank you, Barbara.' The young voice was clear and polite but tinged with withdrawal.

The car started, without Daniel having spoken a word, and slid away smoothly, purring along narrow, green-hedged roads which dreaming elms decorated with wreaths of cool shade. Through the lowered window beside her, Louise caught the distant mocking echo of the cuckoo, hidden among far woods which ran in multi-hued dimness down the sloping sides of a hill a mile away. In past summers she and Daniel had hunted the elusive note from one end of the park to the other and never caught it—like the rainbow's end it always promised, it was always in flight.

Barbara leaned a slim arm on the seat, her silvery coiled hair looped fashionably around her face, openly studying Louise, as if the girl intrigued her. 'Difficult to remember you're seventeen now. In that uniform you could be twelve.' A faint irritation tautened her red mouth. 'You're going to be quite a beauty when you've grown up.' Controlling her impulse of dislike, she gave the girl a hard-edged white smile, her teeth very straight and even. 'Any ideas yet about what you're going to do now you've left school?'

'I thought of going to art school,' Louise told her.

In the driving mirror she caught a flashing, hard look from blue-green eyes, the black brows above them straightening. 'Art school? That's a new idea. Why art school?'

Barbara gave him a quick, narrow-eyed look. 'It sounds fascinating. The best art colleges are in London, of course.'

'I was thinking of St John's College,' Louise said calmly.

'You're too young to live in London alone,' Daniel

rapped abruptly. 'It's out of the question.'

'Daniel, Louise is just the age for London,' said Barbara, spilling bright laughter, her scarlet-nailed hand stroking his arm. 'All the kids adore it, being among people of their own age, having fun, letting their hair down ...'

Daniel did not answer, but in the driving mirror Louise saw his mouth compress and his eyes harden as he stared ahead at the unwinding road as he took a slow bend.

'Is art your favourite subject?' Barbara asked, turning her head back towards Louise. 'Is that what you're really good at?'

'I like it best,' said the cool, soft voice.

'Then there you are,' Barbara said in satisfaction, turning her head towards Daniel again, eyeing his hard profile. 'After all, if it's what she wants ...'

'There's plenty of time to discuss it during the holidays,' Daniel said. 'She's only just come up with the idea. She may change her mind.'

'She ought to be making plans, though,' Barbara said softly.

'She has no need to rush into things!'

'Who's rushing, darling? We're just talking it over. Stop playing the tyrannical big brother and let Louise choose her own future.'

The car put on speed, rushing down a steep hill into the narrow high street of Dower Village, the whitewashed, irregular line of the houses peaceful in the sunlight. Centuries of building had left their mark on the village—from the small clump of modern boxlike houses at the east end to the rambling contours of a medieval house at the west, a thatcher on the pitched roof above it stacking golden switches of reed, his trousers tied with string at the knee.

Cats slept with half-open, glinting eyes on the door-steps. The few shops were drowsily empty of customers. A child wandered along eating an icecream, the only visible inhabitant apart from the thatcher.

Daniel braked. Barbara gave Louise a bright, hard smile, the movement of her mouth never reaching her eyes. 'Come down and browse in the shop when you're bored, won't you? Of course, Queen's Dower is utterly riveting, quite the loveliest house I've ever seen, all that marvellous old furniture—a positive treasure house. But I've no doubt a child of your age gets bored up there with nothing to do.'

Louise made no answer, her blue eyes suddenly brilliant with scorn, although Barbara was not looking at her and missed it. In the driving mirror, however, she caught Daniel's flicking glance and did not hide the feelings she had instinctively experienced as she listened to Barbara.

That chime of high laughter came from Barbara again, her hand moving up Daniel's arm. 'As I've told Daniel, if he's ever short of ready cash, I'd be only too happy to find a buyer for a few pieces from the house. With their background pedigrees I could squeeze a small fortune out of an American dealer for any one of them.'

Louise waited for Daniel to answer, but he made no response, his long hands lying on the wheel, his fingers flexed tensely. Barbara gave him a sideways look, then leaned forward and kissed his cheek. 'Well, I'll be seeing you tonight, darling.' She turned, giving the girl her bright hard smile. 'Daniel has asked me up to dinner—I hope you don't mind, on your first night home, but he thought it would be fun for you to have a private little dinner party, Louise.'

'How nice,' said Louise in her cool, well-mannered voice.

Barbara slid gracefully out of the seat, slammed the door and walked round on to the pavement. Louise flicked a glance up at the small shop whose window was elegantly displaying a dark oak rocking chair across whose wide back a length of glowing poppy-red silk was flung. A white lustre vase made up the display. Eye-catching, simple, yet brilliant, it was the sort of flair which had made Barbara's antique shop famous in the five years since she took over there. Her customers came for miles to visit her. In the summer she attracted many tourists as they drove through the village, including a large number of Americans. She concentrated on quality objects, expensive, rare, highly saleable, and was widely knowledgeable on her subject. Louise had to admit that Barbara knew a good deal about the things she sold, but instinct told her that it was their value in cash rather than intrinsic value which drew the older woman to antiques.

Barbara waved, her slim, elegant figure in the dark dress she wore very graceful. Louise politely lifted a hand as the car spun silently away from the kerb and took the corner out of the village, turning almost immediately into a very narrow, bumpy unmade lane between a wash of white-flowered wild parsley which flowered like lace among a sea of green grass and weeds. The delicate heads of the flowers blew lightly in the breeze of their passing, swaying with the grass around them.

Daniel backed slightly to take the turn into Queen's Dower drive, and Louise said levelly, her tone cool and distant, 'Stop the car, would you, please? I would like to walk up to the house.'

He jerked to a standstill, turning to look at her, his face expressionless, the probe of his blue-green eyes meeting nothing but her unrevealing pale cameo face.

She opened the door and got out, leaving her straw hat on the back seat and depositing her school blazer beside it. Without glancing at him she walked through the gate, propped open with a rough lump of old flint, and strolled into the deep, tranquil shade of a row of horse-chestnuts which still bore the last of their candle-flame flowers, the scent of them nostalgic. She breathed deeply, inhaling the beloved familiar odours. The air was redolent of summer at Queen's Dower, that deep, dusty warm fragrance which grass and flowers, earth and summer leaves made so memorable.

Daniel had not started the car again. He sat, leaning on the wheel, staring after her, and she was strongly aware of the blue-green eyes as she wandered away, her slight body swaying gracefully in the childish blue gingham frock which gave a poignant look of vanishing childhood to her slender limbs, her long silken black hair flowing down her back, the intermittent gleams of sunlight piercing the canopy of leaves above her to give a blackbird gleam to her dark head.

Her eyes moved over the park which surrounded the house, greeting each tree as if it were a familiar old friend. Oaks, elms, beeches, stood at intervals, like resting sentinels, casting dark pools of shade on the sheep-cropped turf. The sheep were scattered throughout the park, grazing ceaselessly, their bent heads tearing at the grass, some lifting mild heads to gaze incuriously at the figure moving among them.

Reaching an ancient cedar tree Louise paused to lean against it, her white throat lifted, her long hair flowing in the summer wind, to stare towards the house as if she greeted a lover. There was a sudden wildness in the blue eyes, a glitter of unshed tears. She pressed her small hands back against the bark of the tree as if drawing sustenance from it. In the weeks since she was last home she had been like a plant uprooted from its native soil and the long homesickness pressed upon her now in a blinding rush.

In the June sunlight Queen's Dower dreamed with all the harmony of a natural object, as if it grew up from the green turf surrounding it, like one of the great oaks. Centuries of building had been coalesced by the slow passage of time, the wearing down of weather, into a warm, mellow unity. Originally built by one of the Norfolk family during the Elizabethan period, in the fashionable shape of an E, it had been added to and altered by successive generations without any of them destroying the perfect line of the building. Leaded diamond windows glittered back at her, reflecting the light of the blue summer sky. Chimneys like barley-sugar sticks twisted up into the air. The gables, dark-timbered, assertive, rose in a harmonious line. Time, eating like moth into the fabric relentlessly, had done so lovingly, softening all irregularities, smoothing them away.

Each time Louise saw it after an absence she was struck dumb, melting with love, aching with it. Beauty struck her like a blow, made her cry. Sensitive, secret, she could no more have allowed anyone to know how she felt about the house than she could have suffered public shame.

While she stood there the long white car slid quietly along the drive and parked in front of the house. Daniel got out. She did not look at him, although she felt his gaze survey her. Aware of his scrutiny, she showed no sign of being even conscious of him, her eyes lifted to the house, her slender body shuddering very slightly as she leaned back against the cedar.

A mistlethrush in beige and white poised a few feet away, head cocked, giving a faint, shivering note of enquiry, his glinting dark eyes shifting in his smooth head.

Daniel leaned on the car, watching her. She stared at the house, slowly beginning to breathe more quietly, the convulsive quivering of her body slowing. She needed time to think, time to be alone. Her bright blue eyes were as cold as jewels in the delicate white beauty of her face as she reluctantly straightened away from the tree and began slowly to walk towards him, her face closed against his scrutiny.

He lifted her case from the boot, slamming it shut, then turned and strode into the house, his hard body violent in motion. In other years Louise had never shut him out from this first moment of seeing the house again. He had known with the intense radar of his long knowledge of her exactly how she felt, what she was thinking, and he had known she had excluded him from the silent glances of loving greeting she had been exchanging with the house. Daniel had always been the one person whom she could bear to know how she felt. Now things were quite changed, and she was not yet certain why.

As she approached the front door Mr and Mrs Duckett came out to meet her, beaming. They had run Queen's Dower for thirty years. They had as much love for the place as either Daniel or Louise, and they treated her as if she were their daughter, rather than the sister of their employer.

'Home again, cherub,' said Mrs Duckett, hugging her into plump warm arms, the tight blue cotton of her dress straining across her chest. Five foot one in her flat brown shoes, she had the Dutch placidity of a doll, her cheeks bright pink, her eyes dark and round, her face full. She smiled easily and often when she loved. When she disliked, her face was hard. As she held Louise away to inspect her, the dark eyes glowed lovingly on the girl's face.

'How are you, Ducky?' Bright blue eyes wore a smile of satisfaction in the reasserted ritual of home-coming. This, at least, was the same. Ducky had always come out to meet the car, with the same words, the same delight in seeing her.

'Come on, let the dog see the rabbit,' Will Duckett said cheerfully, extending his own arms. His wife released her, pushed her towards him, and Louise hugged him, standing on tiptoe to kiss his tough, weathered cheek. As tall as his wife was short, his lanky body wiry with health, he had a bright-eyed ease of manner which she had always found delight-ful. As a small girl she had followed him around the park, watching as he hammered home fencing, sprayed the trees, cut flowers in the formal gardens, mowed the lawns. He had taught her a thousand things about the land, talking continually in his slow West-Country drawl, explaining, expounding, theoris-ing. They had watched the swallows build their nests in the stable yards, rear their fledglings and depart for warmer climes. They had watched the bluebells spring in green spears through the dark earth in the park, flower with the same brilliant blue as Louise's eyes, then slowly fade. He had taught her to fish in the little river which ran along the park boundary, smiling as she excitedly tried to reel in her minute catch, his eyes tender as, wounded unbearably by the gasping of the tiny fish, she had flung it back with a cry of grief.

Now he looked at her from head to toe very slowly, smiling. 'Well, we're growing up, aren't we?'

'You may be,' retorted Louise, her eyes dancing. 'I'm not.'

'He'll never grow up,' said his wife.

'I wouldn't want him to,' said Louise lovingly, and the two of them exchanged a comprehending, smiling look.

They had had no children of their own, a cloud on the blue sky of their long married life, and all their affections had long ago been divided between the house and Louise. Coming to it as a little girl of five, so frail and tiny she was like a black-haired doll, intolerably fragile, she had become an adored pet to both the Ducketts from the first day. When her parents were killed in a car crash three years later, her place in the Ducketts' hearts was cemented for life. Mrs Duckett took over the role of mother to her eagerly, her quiet common sense the stabilising influence which stemmed the spoiling adoration both Will Duckett and Daniel poured out upon her small dark head.

'So you've left school,' said Mrs Duckett, shaking her head. 'Made up your mind what you want to do yet?'

'Don't harry the girl before she's been home five minutes,' Will said in his lazy drawl. 'She'll want to get indoors before you start bullying her!'

Laughing, Louise followed them into the high-vaulted, timbered hall, the centre of the house, great thick walls breathing coolness after the heat of the park. The suits of armour hung upon the walls, the high, arched windows from which dusty sunlight fell lightly, the carved wooden screen hiding the minstrels' gallery, were all unaltered.

Her eyes touched object after object, seeking the eternal verities of life at Queen's Dower, the faded leather gloves in a glass case which had belonged to a Stuart ancestor, the portraits of Georgian members of the family, the poignant silver-handled whip which had been carried by a child who died in the Great Plague in London. Only the faint, sensitive quiver of her pink mouth might have betrayed to a very observant eye that she was deeply disturbed.

The Ducketts waited for her to take in all she needed to, smiling, understanding her perfectly, their fond eyes on the quiet gravity of the oval face. When she turned, a sigh on her lips, Mrs Duckett said, 'You'll want to wash and change after that long journey, cherub. Get out of that old uniform, for a start.'

'Yes, that would be lovely,' said the cool, well-mannered voice which, towards this woman, held unstressed affection and warmth.

'Daniel took your case up,' said Mr Duckett.

Louise left them to return to their own quarters, a converted flint outhouse turned into a charmingly decorative home, and went up the winding stone stair which led to the private family quarters of the house, slowly mounting the hollowed grey steps, aware as she did so that the smooth dip in each had been worn out by the generations of preceding feet. It was a thought which had first come to her years ago, yet each time the singularity of it struck her forcibly, as if she could be aware of the sighing of small ghosts around her on the stairs. The continuity of life at Queen's Dower had a magnetic charm for her.

This was not merely her home; it was a national heritage. The palatial apartments above the hall, unused by the family for years, were shown twice a week to tourists who flocked in great numbers to see them, admiring the house, the beautiful old furniture, the grace and mellow beauty of the green park which held the house as if it were the setting of a jewel.

During the centuries the Norfolk family had fluctuated between power and insignificance, and back again, one generation building an ambitious scheme of intermarriage, wealth and power only to have a succeeding generation somehow evaporate them, as if they were a dandelion clock blown to the winds by a shivering breath. The house held relics which revealed these fluctuations. When the family rose, they bought fine furniture and had portraits painted by the finest artists of the day. When they slowly sank again, the quiet tenor of life flowed back into the house and the daily round of country life resumed its sway. A cruel eighteenth-century Norfolk had brought back japanned cabinets from India, lacquer work and carved ivory. A Victorian recluse had collected thousands of butterflies and moths, exquisitely mounted, which formed now a great exhibition in the open apartments. The one characteristic they had all shared was a bulldog tenacity, a reluctance to part with anything once it came to rest at Queen's Dower. Power, ambition, wealth might come and go, but the beautiful possessions it had brought them somehow remained in their tenacious grip.

The tourists could not know, of course, of the permanent struggle Daniel Norfolk had now to keep the house exactly as it had always been.

The cost of maintaining Queen's Dower was a drain upon his income. Several farms occupied by tenants were attached to the house, Daniel ran a company in Bristol which imported various foreign goods, but the profits from all this poured into Queen's Dower as if it were water soaking into the rich earth. Daniel dressed well, drove a good car, but every penny he could spare was engrossed by the house, and he spent all his free time at home, indifferent to the lures of a more luxurious way of life.

The Ducketts had help from the village each day. Three women came up for a few hours in the morning to work in the house. Will Duckett had two casual part-time workers in the gardens and park. The wife of the local vicar eagerly acted as guide to the house on open days in the summer, ekeing out her own small income with what Daniel could pay her.

The constant, nagging struggle to keep the house afloat was always present in all their minds, sometimes aggravated by sudden unexpected disasters, as when one of the chimneys showed signs of collapse and had to be hurriedly repaired, or when one winter a burst water pipe flooded the exquisite Chinese carpets in the White Lady's Room, a bedroom in the open apartments dominated by a portrait of a lady in a white silk dress.

How much longer Daniel could contrive to hold the balance Louise dreaded to think.

She turned along a long passage, floored with tough matting, then opened a door at the end, marked

Private, and went through into the family part of the house.

Her own bedroom was at the end of the east wing, occupying the top of the red brick castellated tower which formed the final flourish of the wing, lined with tiny windows which glinted in the sunlight. It was octagonal, and the strangeness of that gave it magic, making it a unique and special place to her ever since she was a child. In this room she had read the old fairy stories, placing them all here, with herself as heroine.

Daniel had furnished it for her several years ago, choosing a diminutive Victorian print in eggshell blue flowers for the wallpaper, with curtains of a deeper shade to set it off, and a carpet of deep white pile. The centre of the room was, as it had always been, a small fourposter bed, originally made for a daughter of the house in the seventeenth century. Her portrait in soft yellow satin hung in the open apartments, her lustrous dark eyes wistful. At seventeen she had married a savage, cruel aristocrat who had given her three children before her twenty-first birthday. She had died at the third birth. Louise always thought of her sadly as she lay in the bed. The curtains matched those at the windows, and the heavy white silk quilt on the bed shimmered in the sunlight as if it were water.

For a few moments she stood in the centre of the room, looking around her, feeling the dear familiarity soak into her, then she sighed and began to unpack her case.

Pulling out a childish, thin cotton dressing-gown she turned and went out of the room. It was relaxing to stand under a cool shower, feeling the fine needles of water strip away the dust and fatigue of the journey. She would not let herself think for the moment. Ever since she met Daniel on the station platform something had been eating bitterly away at the back of her mind, but she kept it at bay. Slowly she turned round, feeling the coolness of the water trickling down her heated skin.

Drying herself slowly, she slid into the dressing-gown. It had two buttons missing and she grimaced, thinking that it was time she bought a new one. It had done well enough for school, where she had rarely needed to use it, and it was an ingrained habit to be thrifty if she could, knowing how much money was needed for the house.

When she halted in the doorway of her own room she saw Daniel leaning against the fourposter, his arms folded, a frown on his handsome face.

As she stood framed in the doorway she looked gravely at him. The sunlight streaming in from the corridor windows outlined her slender body more clearly than she knew, the thin cotton almost transparent in the light, moulding her small high breasts and tiny waist, the fine rounded curves of hips and thighs.

Daniel stared through lowered lids, his eyes dropping over her body, a faint flush coming into his hard face. 'You need a new dressing-gown,' he said harshly.

'I know,' she said. 'This one only just fits and I've had it for two years.'

'You must be growing out of most of your clothes. You'd better go into Bristol and do some shopping. Barbara would go along and advise you.'

Louise moved forward, her face cool, unaware that her movements sent the edges of the dressing-gown folding back, the missing buttons forcing the material to float loosely. Daniel's strange blue-green eyes did not miss the brief glimpse of slim white thighs. Thrusting his hands into his pockets he turned away and walked to the window with his back to her.

'I would prefer to buy my own clothes, thank you, Daniel,' she said politely. 'I think I'm past the age when someone else chooses what I wear.'

He turned his head to look at her. 'Just as you like.'

She had pinned her long black hair on top of her head during the shower, and the severity of the change had given her face a more emphasised purity of outline. The smooth white skin of neck and face had a pearly glimmer. Despite the childish, faded cotton gown her beauty was compelling, and Daniel looked at her between his half-lowered lids, his eyes glinting over her, then restlessly moved to another window, staring out over the green shade of the park. His back to her, he said, 'I hadn't meant to bring Barbara to meet you, but she saw me drive through the village and insisted on coming along.'

'How kind of her,' the polite, gentle voice said without expression. Underneath the calm exterior of her face her mind was working feverishly, but none of it showed in her eyes or face. She leaned as he had done on the polished dark wood shaft of the fourposter, her slender body relaxed against it, one hand very small and white against the dark wood, her legs stretched out, feet bare, the childlike gown giving the slender curves of her body poignancy.

'Daniel, have you thought any more about asking Sally Blare and her brother to stay here for a few weeks? After all, I stayed with her last Easter and I

seem a lifetime away . . .'

'I'm not Methuselah,' he said sharply, his brows a black line.

'Thirty-five next birthday, isn't it?' she asked. 'If you cast your mind back to when you were my age, maybe you'll remember just how old one can feel at seventeen.'

His eyes narrowed on her face, searching it. 'I remember very well, as it happens,' he said, but absently, as if something else was preoccupying him.

She gave him a sudden teasing smile, her blue eyes very bright. 'Was she pretty?'

His face altered. His mouth dented humorously, his eyes smiling down at her. 'Very,' he said softly.

'Blonde like Barbara?'

'What makes you guess that?'

'You always choose blondes,' she said, tongue in cheek.

'What do you know about my preferences?' he scoffed.

Her eyes lifted to his face again, a curious brightness in them, then slid away again. 'I've never seen you with a dark girl.'

The silence between them was charged. She could feel it in every nerve of her body, a curious, tremulous pulsing awareness.

Soon after her parents' death she had awoken from a nightmare one evening and run in misery to find Daniel, only to halt with a shocked gasp to find him with a very pretty blonde girl on the sofa, kissing her.

After that one horrified stare, she had run out again, in her long nightdress, and kept running, almost unable to think or be sure what was wrong with her, until she found herself in one of the unused rooms at the top of the house, crouching in the dusty darkness, sobbing. Daniel had found her and carried her back to bed, holding her gently. He had said nothing about the incident, but never again had he brought any of his girl-friends back to Queen's Dower while Louise was at home. Louise had been aware that he had women friends. They all merged for her now into one image, a sophisticated blonde with Barbara's expertly made up features and good grooming. They had come and gone in the years between, and as one succeeded another she had ceased to regard them as individuals, accepting them as Daniel's occasional companions without ever taking them seriously.

For a week after that night she had stared at him with hurt, wild blue eyes, holding him at a distance, rejecting all his overtures with childish dignity. Only gradually had she forgiven him.

Oddly, Daniel said, 'What about your preferences, then? In this thinking about marriage you've been doing, what sort of husband have you decided you want?'

She shrugged, her mouth dimpling. 'Rich, handsome and sexy.' The dark lashes flickered teasingly, and the blue eyes laughed up at him. It was the standard reply all her friends gave to the question which had been in their minds for months. As the time for leaving school came nearer their talk of jobs, life, love, had grown more intense and engrossing.

Daniel did not laugh back. His hand moved from her elbow to her chin, tilting her head. The laughter died in her eyes and a curious, startled expression arose in them. He stared down at her, his eyes hard and intent, almost accusing.

'That isn't funny,' he said. 'What would a child of your age know about men? You're barely old enough to have known any but me.'

Louise looked secretive, her lashes fluttering down. 'We have weekly dances at the school. Didn't you know? The boys from Granwich College come over every Saturday.'

Daniel's mouth was sardonic. 'And have you been experimenting with a few flirtations with these schoolboy Romeos, Louise?'

'What do you think?' Her eyes danced, intrigue in them. 'Of course, the teachers hang around and chaperone us.' The little dimple appeared in her cheek, and her mouth curved. 'But you'd be amazed to know the amount of secret kissing that goes on in the school passages. We take it in turns to sneak off while the teachers aren't looking.'

His face held no amusement, his eyes glinting over her face. There was a silence. 'Sally Blare's brother is at Granwich, isn't he?'

'He's leaving this year,' she agreed calmly. 'He's got five A levels . . . two better than me. Peter's clever.'

'And what is clever Peter going to do now he's left?' Daniel asked, his fingers hardening on her chin.

She looked demure. 'He's going to an art school in London,' she said softly.

The silence brought her eyes to his face, the wild blue of them filled with mockery.

His face was unreadable.

'An interesting coincidence,' he said after a moment.

Louise didn't answer.

'He is the reason for your sudden decision to go to London art school, I take it?' he pressed.

She smiled sweetly. 'He's rather good-looking, and ...' Her eyes lowered, a secretive look in her face, and she cut off the rest.

'And what?' Daniel demanded, his eyes probing the smooth contours of her averted face.

'Nothing.'

'Finish it,' he insisted, his fingers slightly shaking her chin.

'You'll laugh,' she said softly.

'I hope I will,' he retorted between his teeth, very grim.

She flickered a look at him then, her eyes a brilliant, blinding blue. 'He thinks he's in love with me,' she said.

This time the silence was unmistakably charged with electric menace. She did not look up again, her lashes still.

'His parents are certainly rich,' he said tersely. 'He's a good-looking boy, apparently, on your testimony. What about your third requirement, Louise? How does he match up there?'

The blue eyes remained hidden, the mouth curving in a little smile. 'He improves on closer acquaintance,' she said.

Dark hot colour swept suddenly into Daniel's face. The blue-green eyes stared down at her, hard with anger. She looked up suddenly, deliberately, and their eyes met in a long stare.

'Are you deliberately needling me?' he asked grimly.

'Why should my love life needle you, my dear brother?' she asked him sweetly.

His mouth compressed. 'Love life!' he said tersely. 'You're nothing but a child.'

Her smile was tantalising. 'Am I?'

Their glances locked again, hers softly amused, his probing, as if he was trying to discover something she was hiding from him.

'I've changed a lot in the last six months,' she said. 'Don't tell me you hadn't noticed.'

His eyes swept over her in the clinging cotton gown. 'I'd noticed,' he said tersely.

'I thought you had,' she said, her mouth curved.

'What's that supposed to mean?'

She shifted her ground, feeling it unstable under her feet. 'Are you going to let me invite Sally and Peter here?'

His face was irritated. 'Why on earth do you want anyone? You've always been perfectly happy until this year. I'd been planning a long, peaceful summer.'

'Just you and me and Barbara?' she suggested, tongue in cheek.

Daniel stared at her intently then. 'Barbara will make no difference to us, she'll be busy at the shop all day. In the evenings she could come up and have dinner with us. I thought it might be nice for you to have another female around the place in the evenings.'

She surveyed him calmly. 'She's hardly my age group. In fact, she tends to patronise me, and I don't enjoy being patronised.'

'When the summer is over you could start at art school in Bristol,' he suggested. 'You would meet plenty of people of your own age there.'

'It would be nice to have Peter and Sally here, though,' she said. 'I promised Peter I would show him the best places to fish ...'

'If you think I'm standing around here watching you experiment with young Blare you can think again,' he snapped, suddenly so angry that he lost control of his temper.

The blue eyes glittered in sudden triumph as they read the look on his face. 'Jealous, Daniel?' she asked softly.

The bones seemed to push out from beneath the brown skin, making his face all angles, a dangerous menacing mask. The blue-green eyes flashed at her savagely. For a second he didn't move, his jaw tight, poised on the point of violent movement, yet holding himself in check.

Louise laughed, and the mocking little sound, uttered quite deliberately, snapped the leash of his control.

He caught her shoulders in hands that did not care if they hurt, dragging her towards him. Without resistance she lifted her face and felt his glittering eyes on her mouth for a second or two before his hard mouth came down hungrily to take it, as if he had needed to do so for a long time, was urgently in need of the feel and taste of it under his lips. Novice, quivering, her lips parted under his hot exploration, her arms slid slowly round his neck, pulling his head down, her fingers pressing against the dark hair, her slender body melting against him. She felt the shudder of intolerable necessity that ran through him. His hands moved down her, shaping the curved, slender outline, his palms warm against her skin through the thin cotton.

She had been kissed before, by boys of her own age, as she had told him; fumbling experiments lasting a few moments in the school passages, shy, slightly nervous, unsatisfactory. This was totally different.

There was a smothering silence between them as if

both had ceased to be at all capable of coherent thought. Under Daniel's demanding caresses she was yielding entirely, her slender body plastic in his arms, giving him what the shaking of his hands, the unsated demand of his mouth told her he wanted.

Her heart was running wild under his moving hands, and the response she was giving him was unfettered, total.

Breathing thickly, he suddenly pulled his head back, his mouth detaching itself from the soft lips as if he had to use force to make himself leave them. His face was darkly flushed, his eyes leaping wildly.

'My God, no ... Louise ... no!' He said the words as if he had to convince himself rather than her.

She looked at him without speaking, brilliance in her eyes, a passionate bloom on the mouth his hot kiss had been consuming with such unleashed hunger. He ran his fingers through his hair, staring down at her as if he had never seen her before.

'It's madness,' he said huskily. 'I'm twice your age ... you're too innocent to realise ... We've been so close for so long. I've taught you to ride and swim and drive a car, I've been your whole family for so many years. I can't take advantage of your affection for me. It would be criminal!' He ended almost bitterly, then spun on his heel and strode out of the room.

After a long moment, Louise moved to the bed and lay down on the white silk quilt, uncaring if she crumpled it, her whole body trembling. Stretching out an arm, she picked up a photograph from her bedside table and looked at it with loving eyes. It was a wedding group. At the centre stood a woman of thirty who any eye could see bore a close resemblance to

Louise. Beside her stood a tall man of fifty, his smile warm, his eyes gentle. After smiling at their faces, Louise glanced tenderly at the young man in a morning suit and carnation, his lean face wearing a faint smile as he looked down at the little girl whose shoulders he held. Herself, at five, in a bridesmaid's dress of blue silk and lace, as delicately fragile as a flower petal, all pale skin and huge incandescent blue eyes, staring into the camera solemnly, yet with her cheek slightly bent to touch Daniel's hand upon her shoulder.

She felt tears prick, remembering as if it had been yesterday. She had never known her own father. He had died when she was six months old. When her mother married Daniel's father, she had begged to be bridesmaid, eager to wear a pretty dress, and both Daniel and his father had smiled on her with adoring agreement. From the very first she had been the centre of the household. An only child, Daniel had been amused and touched by her openly expressed adoration of him. Her frail beauty as a child had made him protective. The three years of marriage between their parents had passed in a whirl of golden happiness. It had been Daniel who had had to break the news of the car crash to her, holding her on his lap, his arms comforting, his cheek against her hair.

The storm of tears which shook her had shaken him, too. He had kissed her wet little face, his mouth warm on her wet eyelids, closing the wild blue eyes. 'Don't, darling,' he had whispered. 'I'll always be here ... you belong to me now.'

She had gone to sleep with that promise as her comfort, her face worn to a white glaze by tears, and as the long years of her childhood passed in the sleepy security of Queen's Dower Daniel's whispered words had taken on for her the proportions of an oath.

Daniel belonged to her; it was an unquestioned fact. Even when he sent her away to boarding school, their minds and hearts remained invisibly linked. When she returned home, they flew into each other's arms in unashamed delight. He never grew bored with her presence. He sought her company tirelessly. The hours they spent together in retrospect had the radiant sunshine of a dream, except that the dream had the solidity of reality behind it.

It had never entered her head that Daniel might marry. She had not been jealous of his women friends except on the night when she saw him with the blonde in his arms, and then, awaking from a nightmare, she had felt a physical impact of pain, as if he had deserted her when she needed him. Daniel had known: she knew that. He had said nothing, but his eyes had been curiously anxious, apologetic, as if he had been caught in an act of infidelity, and women had ceased to visit the house to see him. If he had girl-friends he was careful Louise should never know.

When her love for him grew from that of an adoring younger sister into that of a girl fast approaching womanhood, she did not know.

It had come home to her when he took her to a fair during the last half-term break. While she rode on a gaudy yellow chicken, her hair flying wildly around her face, Daniel had gone to buy her an icecream and she had fallen into conversation with a boy on the next animal. He had flirted with her, saying outrageous things which made her laugh. Then she had

seen Daniel staring at them. Before the roundabout
had slowed to a stop he had thrown away the icecream he held, his hands hard as he pulled her down
beside him. Astonished, she caught the angry, jealous
glare of his eyes at the boy, who had flinched, vanishing. Without a word Daniel had stalked out of the
fairground, pulling her after him, his hand hurting
her wrist.

'Don't ever talk to strangers like that again,' he had
snapped, pushing her into the car, his face harsh.

'No, Daniel,' she had said submissively, and for a
second he had looked at her, his eyes filled with restless fire.

The incident had awoken her. She had felt no sense
of urgency, aware that she had to end her schooldays,
and still dreamily content with their old warm, loving
relationship.

Then that day on the platform she had felt a
change in him, an indefinable withdrawal which
puzzled her. Seeing Barbara with him had increased
her bewilderment. He had never brought someone
else with him to meet her before; their first moments
together after an absence were too precious. She had
known it was a form of declaration, a silent statement
of intent, and what he had just said explained it.
Daniel had decided he had no right to make any claim
on her. He was disturbed both by the gap between
their ages, and by the possibility that she might be
misled by old affection into mistaking her feelings
for him. She saw that he had decided to stand aside,
to shut her out, in order to free her to find some more
suitable man of an age near her own. A faint smile
touched her mouth. Yet the moment she had shown
signs of interest in Peter Blare, Daniel had reacted

with the same jealous, savage possessiveness he had shown before. Louise lay back, her arms under her head, her body limply relaxed, and a curious smile lit her blue eyes.

CHAPTER TWO

BARBARA looked like a glittering dream as she joined them that evening. The straight, uncluttered silver shift she wore flamed as her body moved, and she had silvered her nails on hands and feet, making the sultry plum colour of her lipstick somehow startling and novel. Through her dark lashes Louise considered her coolly. She was beautiful, there was no doubt about that, and she had taste—of a kind. She had flair and chic, but when she looked at the delicately chased silver on the table, her dark eyes narrowing in appreciation, it sent a shiver down Louise's back to hear her say, 'George I ... very nice, darling. They're worth twice as much as the ones I bought last week. I sold those to an American yesterday, by the way.'

Daniel looked politely interested, but Louise could not raise a flicker of interest, wondering silently how someone who knew as much as Barbara about beautiful objects, and who had such an eye for colour and line, could only see such things in terms of money.

Before Barbara had arrived, Daniel had been stiffly silent, his whole attitude quite obviously evasive. Louise had made no attempt to speak to him, sitting quietly in her chair, sipping a half full glass of sherry which he had given her reluctantly.

Barbara looked across the table at her, her eyes flickering with amused contempt over the simple little blue dress she was wearing. 'Dan, darling, shouldn't the child have some new clothes? Goodness, that thing looks almost identical to her school uniform.'

Louise did not glance towards him, aware of the quick, brief look he was giving her, unaware of the delicate fragility of her slender body in the colour which echoed the shade of her eyes, unaware of the sensual impact of her bare white nape and the mass of her black hair wreathed on top of her head. She felt suddenly helplessly young, unable to cope with either of them, a sting of tears at the back of her eyes.

Barbara was talking again, laughing, telling some anecdote about a sale she had made which had a faint flavour of dishonesty about it. Daniel seemed barely to notice, a polite smile on his hard mouth, his eyes on the bowl of fruit in the centre of the table.

'You're very quiet,' said Barbara, turning to her. 'Tired after the journey home?'

Louise seized on the excuse thankfully. 'Actually, I've got a terrible headache,' she said, putting down her napkin. 'Would you think me very rude if I asked to be excused? Train journeys sometimes give me a migraine, and I'm really not very hungry.'

Barbara's smile was a flash of white teeth and that smouldering lipstick. 'Of course not, my dear . . . why didn't you say? Heavens, you really look quite white.'

Louise stood up. 'Goodnight,' she said vaguely, halfway between them both.

Daniel murmured something incoherent. His eyes followed her as she walked out of the room, then Barbara put a hand towards him, smiling.

'Poor little thing, she looks quite worn out.'

Louise closed the door and escaped to her room. She sat on her bed staring at the curtains blowing softly to and fro in the warm night air.

Ducky came in clucking softly. 'What's all this about migraine? Why didn't you tell me?' She peered into the white little face under the black hair. 'Yes, you look terrible. Why aren't you lying down? You know there's only one way you can get rid of these migraines—a good sleep, that's what you need. Too much excitement, coming home, that's the trouble.' While she talked she was gently helping Louise out of her clothes and pushing her into a knee-length pink cotton nightdress with a high neckline threaded with white ribbons which tied flutteringly at the throat. Ducky loosened her hair, brushed it carefully, tenderly, until it lay in a silken stream down her back, smiling at her as she stood back with the conscious, satisfied look of an artist regarding his best work.

'Now you look ready for bed,' she said, tucking her in between the sheets. 'Off to sleep, now. You'll feel better in the morning.'

'Goodnight, Ducky,' Louise said faintly as the door closed, and then she let the tears which had been threatening all evening come bursting out of her aching eyes.

She cried without making a sound, terrified of being overheard. She heard the grandfather clock in the passage sonorously striking the hour just as she was on the point of falling asleep, and woke with a jerk, like a train which was just descending a dark tunnel but was braked abruptly. Her nerves jangled and she lay, eyes wide open, staring into the darkness. Then she heard the voices. Barbara was leaving. Louise climbed out of bed silently and went to the window. A few moments later she saw Daniel climb into Barbara's car. Her body stiffened as she stared down at the top of his black head. The car shot away down the drive.

She stood at the window, shivering in the night air, for so long that her feet went to sleep and cramp suddenly caught her off guard, sending a crunching wave of pain through her muscles. Angrily she turned away from the window and sat down on her bed. Jealousy made an acrid taste in her mouth. She wrapped herself in the silk quilt, uncaring if she crumpled it. He was with Barbara ... the grandfather clock chimed a single deep note. One o'clock. Daniel had been gone for two hours. Like a witch in the silent darkness Louise sat, her eyes slanting bitterly, angrily, and waited.

It was three in the morning when she heard his slow footstep on the drive, and she went to the window to look down at him, her blue eyes wild with jealousy and anger. He was walking very slowly, as if he were exhausted, his head bent. Suddenly he glanced up directly at the tower room. Louise shot back from the window, but she was sure he had seen her.

Had he even wanted her to see him? Was it part of his plan to make her realise that she could never enter his adult world, be his equal? She was a child, totally inexperienced, innocent, and Daniel was a man twice her age. When she was born he was already older than she was now ... the thought made her wince. Daniel had been as old as Peter Blare, she thought. An eighteen-year-old boy, perhaps having already fallen in love. The vast abyss between them was a dark one, all the years during which she had been passing through childhood and he had been a man in a man's world. While she played with her dolls and learnt to read, what had Daniel had to amuse himself and occupy his time? She gritted her teeth, considering it in a way she had never done before.

He kissed me, she thought, her heart flickering in excited pain. He was jealous when I talked about Peter. Then she thought, sickeningly, so what? Does it even mean what I thought it meant? He has always loved me, but as his litle sister, the only family he has ever had for years. I'm in love with him, but how do I know he feels anything like that for me?

Then her body reminded her and hot colour flowered in her cheeks, as she remembered the desire she had felt in him, the shaking of his hands as he slowly slid them over her.

Even that, her cool mind said firmly, doesn't mean he feels the same way, the way I want him to feel. She wasn't that innocent. Desire and love were not the same.

Forcing herself to go back to bed, she lay down, her limbs chilled. In the morning, she thought, she would ring Sally and invite her to come. Sally had said she would come the moment she got the call. Sally was desperately keen to visit Queen's Dower. Louise had never invited anyone from school before; she had never wanted to. Daniel had been enough for her and she had wanted nothing but him.

Suddenly she heard his footsteps in the passage, soft on the carpet. She felt him halt at her door. He stood there, and she sensed that he was listening to the sound of her breathing. She tried to slow it to a sleep rhythm, hard though it was when her pulses were leaping wildly. A strange brushing sound puzzled her. What was he doing? Then he moved away and she heard him in the bathroom, very faintly.

After a few moments she heard his bedroom door close.

It was hard to lie there knowing he was so close. They were alone in the apartments at night. Long ago Mrs Duckett had given up sleeping in the family rooms. For a while, after Louise's mother died, she had stayed close to her at night, but after a while she had returned to her own quarters, since Louise was perfectly happy with Daniel close at hand if she needed him. During the day, the Ducketts were around all the time. It had not seemed necessary to Daniel to have anyone in the family rooms during the night, since Louise was at boarding school so much of the year.

She got up very early, showered and dressed in riding clothes, then snatched a glass of milk and an apple from the kitchen and went off to the stables. Her mare, Velvet, looked at her from mysterious slanting eyes, breathing lovingly into her hand as she fed her the apple. Louise leant her head against the silky coat, running a hand down the loose mane. Velvet was glad to see her again, turning a graceful head to nuzzle her.

She rode into the park, staring up into the milky morning sky, seeing the blue shimmering deep within the early mist. The grass was dew-sprinkled and the air had a cool fresh scent.

She heard Daniel's tall grey gelding coming over the turf before she saw it, and reined Velvet, turning to watch him. He joined her and they stared at each other warily.

It was another break with tradition. Always they met in the kitchen and went out to the stables together to saddle their horses before they rode. Only this time it had been her decision to break the mould of their years together

'We've got to talk together,' he said flatly.

She felt Velvet stirring restlessly, impatient of the delay. Her black head turned away and she gave him no answer, giving Velvet the little prod with her heels which was the signal to go. Velvet broke into a gentle trot, then began to canter easily, her slender legs covering the ground gracefully. Daniel sat back watching them, holding his own mount back. On the elegant little mare's back, Louise moved as if she were part of her mount, her slender body in the plain white silk shirt erect, her hair flying back from her head like a black silk banner.

Daniel came after her at last and they rode hard, his gelding in hot pursuit, gaining at last, far too powerful for Velvet, passing them with Daniel's sardonic, pointed glance at Louise a flash of blue-green eyes and hard mouth.

On a low hillock he paused, watching a flight of crows from a nearby field, their black bodies ungainly as they landed and began to squabble.

Louise saw him dismount and leave his horse to graze, flinging himself down on the grass. Reluctantly she joined him, flinging herself down in the same casual fashion. He had his arms crossed under his head. His eyes stared up into the sky which was growing a deep, bright blue. The night mist had cleared as they rode.

'The grass is damp,' she said.

Daniel turned his head, and she felt his eyes flick over her. Boyish in the biscuit jodhpurs and silk shirt, she nervously picked a piece of grass and chewed it, feeling the green sap spring into her mouth, bitter and fresh.

'I want to apologise for yesterday,' he said, looking back up at the sky. 'I lost my temper. The trouble is, Louise, you've changed, and the little girl I've known for so long has vanished for good. I suppose I have to get used to that idea.'

'It doesn't matter,' she said, not knowing what else to say.

'It damned well does,' he said, suddenly angry. 'My God, if someone else had behaved to you the way I did, I'd be bloody mad ... even though you're growing up fast, you're still a kid.'

She plucked another piece of grass, her fingers trembling. 'Let's forget it,' she said with a pretence of lightness. 'May I have Sally and Peter to stay?'

He sat up, looking down at her, his eyes accusing. 'I explained yesterday—I wanted to have this last summer. It may well be our last as it always was ... I thought you would want that too. Don't ruin it.'

'It's already ruined,' she sighed, meeting his eyes.

'Because of what I did?' His face flushed darkly.

'No,' she said quietly. 'Because things have already changed too much. You can't put the clock back, Daniel. I'm not a little girl any more. My childhood summers at Queen's Dower are over.'

He breathed harshly, staring at her. Then he got up and caught his gelding, mounting easily. 'Very well, do as you damned well please,' he said bitterly, turning the horse. His hoofs thundered back towards the house.

Louise took her time in returning to the house, her eyes thoughtful. When she had eaten a light breakfast of toast and orange juice, she rang Sally.

'Oh, super,' Sally breathed, ecstatic at the prospect. 'For two whole weeks? Daddy will be thrilled. I told him you'd invited us and he was tickled pink. He said he'd drive us down himself.'

Louise made a face, knowing the polite response. 'He must stay to lunch, then. Daniel will be thrilled to see him.'

'Peter will be thrilled to see *you*,' Sally breathed. 'As if you didn't know! He's definitely crazy about you, angel.'

Louise laughed. Behind her she heard Daniel walk into the sitting-room and said softly, 'I'm crazy about Peter, too.'

Sally giggled. 'I must rush off and tell him. Do you want to talk to him?'

'Not now,' said Louise, conscious of Daniel's stare. She rang off and turned, defiant, still in jodhpurs and shirt. Daniel's mouth was derisive.

'Young love,' he said nastily, smiling in a way which she had never seen him do before. 'Touching.'

'Their father is driving them down. I've asked him to lunch.'

'Charming,' he said, his mouth like a trap. 'I find the man as fascinating as a box full of spiders.'

'I'm sure you'll be the perfect host,' she said coolly. 'He's always wanted to be invited to Queen's Dower.'

'I'm aware of that,' Daniel snapped. 'If I'd wanted him here I would have invited him myself.'

'Sorry,' she shrugged. 'I couldn't avoid it.'

'You mean you did it to annoy me,' he said bitingly. 'Any weapon will do, won't it, Louise?'

'Why should I want to annoy you?' she asked, raising an eyebrow.

'Do you think I'm blind to the fact that you get an adolescent thrill out of needling me?' he asked coldly. 'Like most females, you love to exercise your power on every male within sight.'

She stared in stunned disbelief. Suddenly he was an enemy, sniping at her with complete disregard for her feelings.

'Is that what I'm doing?' she asked, summoning all her courage to defy him.

'Isn't it?' His eyes flashed. 'Last night you drove me to do something damned stupid ...'

'I did nothing of the kind!'

He moved closer, staring furiously down into her face. 'Do you think it's easy for me to accept the fact that the little girl I've taught to ride and swim and play tennis is now ready to learn something more adult?'

Her skin burned, but her blue eyes remained lifted to his face. 'I can't help what's happening to me.'

'No,' he said bitterly, 'It's as natural as the buds breaking on the oak trees, but I've put in too many years on you, Louise, to find it easy to step aside and watch from the sidelines while another man teaches you what it means to be a woman.'

Her heart was beating so fast she was nerveless. Huskily, she said, 'Daniel, I ...' Her hand reached out towards him, but he moved back as if the touch of it might burn him.

'No,' he said harshly. 'I'm not putting this too well, I realise that. It has to be said, though, so for God's sake listen.' He took a deep breath, shoving his hands into his pockets. 'We've been very close—closer than the average brother and sister, I imagine. I'm all the family you've had since you were tiny. Now that you're growing up it isn't strange that you should feel ...' He hesitated, his face restless. 'Let's say a little interested in me ... most adolescents have crushes on someone much older. There's nothing new in that.'

Her face grew crimson. 'A crush on you!' He made it sound so meaningless, a brief childish infatuation which bore no resemblance to the way she really felt.

'Call it what you like, the truth is we both know that all the needling and provocation which has been coming from your direction lately has its basis in something of the kind.'

She stood very still, biting her lower lip, staring at his angry face with a sensation of bitterness.

'I'm flattered,' he went on in a tone which implied the opposite. 'It isn't so surprising, though, considering how close we've always been. They say girls always adore their fathers before they start looking beyond them for their own young men ... I suppose the same thing applies for us.'

'Thanks for the psycho-analysis,' she said tartly.

His eyes narrowed. 'Don't talk to me like that. I'm trying to get us back on an even keel. I can't stand much more of this.'

'I'm sorry if I've embarrassed you,' she snapped.

Daniel's face darkened. 'For God's sake, I'm no more immune to the sort of invitations you've been throwing out lately than any other young man would be. I'm a man with normal instincts and you've suddenly turned into a ravishing girl. You've been my property for so long that I find it hard to stand back. You saw that months ago, don't pretend you didn't. You realised you could make me react in a new way—

you got me to show jealousy at that bloody fair-ground, and ever since you've been using your new-found powers on me ... well, I'm telling you now, it's got to stop!'

'I'm sorry if I find you a little contradictory,' she said very coldly. 'You seem to be telling me to find myself a boy of my own age, yet at the same time you get angry every time I show signs of being inter-ested in one.'

His eyes flared, his mouth tightening. 'My God, you never learn, do you? Haven't you listened to a word I said? All right, Louise. I'm as confused as you are. My brain tells me that now is the time for me to get out of your life and let you find someone more suitable, but I've been so involved with you since you were five years old that I find it damned hard to do what I know I should do.'

She looked at him, suddenly saddened and a little lost, sensing the sincerity of what he said.

His face softened at the expression on her oval face. 'Darling, we've both got a lot to learn. The very last thing I want is to wake up and find you my enemy. I want to find the path through this labyrinth, if I can, and you've got to be as aware of what's going on as I am. When you were tiny I used to read you fairy stories, remember?'

She nodded, her mouth quivering.

'Everything was so simple in that world. Black was black and white was white, people were good or evil, and there was no problem which couldn't be solved. Well, life isn't like that. It's neither black nor white, it's grey. We all make mistakes, we all get confused. At the moment, I'm as confused as you are, darling. You seem to alter from one minute to the next.' His blue-green eyes were gentle. 'Like an image in a fairground mirror, you dissolve in front of my eyes ... from my little Louise into this new Louise, half woman, half child. I never know which I will see.'

'Neither do I,' she admitted, smiling ruefully. 'Curious, isn't it?'

He put a hand to her black hair, his fingers caressing. 'Very curious ... Alice in Wonderland curious ... You know I love you, Louise ... child or woman, whichever you are at the moment ... but we've both got to accept that things aren't the way they were. I was behaving like an ostrich with my head in the sand when you arrived. I thought we could have a last summer together, just as we always used to, but it's already too late. I realise that now.'

'We could try,' she said faintly, gazing at him.

He shook his head. 'No. It wouldn't work. Just try to remember what I've said. Lay off the deliberate needling ... I've discovered I've got a hair-trigger temper where you're concerned. Let's try to be adult about it all. In later years we'll laugh together over it, and you'll be glad you listened to me.'

She lowered her lashes. 'Yes, Daniel,' she said submissively, as she so often had before.

He looked at her restlessly. 'Look, how about driving into Bristol? I've got work to do, and you could do shopping. I'll pick you up at around six and we'll have dinner in town together.' His eyes teased her. 'Very grown up and formal dinner. Would you like that?'

'Yes, please, Daniel,' she said eagerly.

'Come on, then,' he invited. 'You can buy some of those clothes we've been talking about ... go mad, if you want to. I can always go bankrupt and sell Queen's Dower.'

She laughed and went upstairs to change.

She spent the whole of the afternoon choosing a new wardrobe. It was not, in fact, as expensive as Daniel no doubt imagined it would be, since she deliberately exercised care that it should not be, but her own sense of what suited her made her very difficult to please. When she met him at six she was wearing one of her new dresses, a full-skirted, tight-waisted white dress made of fine strawcloth, with a scooped-out neckline which emphasised the high swell of her breasts and the long pale neck.

Daniel glanced towards her, his face polite, then visibly did a double take, his eyes narrowing, as if he were shaken by what he saw.

Louise threaded her way through the tables of the café where they had met and sat down beside him, laying her purchases on the free chair beside her. Then she looked at him calmly, smiling.

'I haven't bankrupted you,' she said lightly.

'Haven't you?' he asked in a dry voice, still staring at her.

She began to pour out the tea he had already ordered, avoiding the hard stare of his blue-green eyes.

'Do you like my new dress?' she asked, flicking a glance at him as she passed his cup.

He made no answer, his mouth hard, but there was sarcasm in the opalescent eyes.

She flushed slightly, sipping her tea to cover her nervous awareness of him.

'I thought that instead of having dinner in Bristol we might drive into Weston-super-Mare,' he said after a moment. 'We could get some sea air and stroll along the promenade before dinner.'

'I'd love that,' she said easily.

'You always loved the sea,' he said, nostalgia in his tone. 'You used to go white with excitement when we were driving to Weston, remember? Couldn't wait to get out on the beach and see the waves washing up on the sand ...'

'I remember you once built me a sandcastle so enormous it was big enough for me to sit in.' Her eyes danced. 'You filled the moat with water and I sailed a boat on it until the water all drained away into the sand.' It was sad to remember that, the regret she had felt as the browny yellow sand slowly absorbed all the water, just as time had absorbed the warmth and closeness which had once been between her and Daniel.

Their eyes met and a similar regret flew between them, then he looked away, his face closing into a mask.

They drove out of Bristol through the green countryside along the Weston road, past shady woods and pastures full of cows, leaving behind them the Avon gorge with its red cliffs and dark foliaged trees.

Weston-super-Mare was filled with tourists. The streets were gay with holiday atmosphere, buckets and spades, paper flags, souvenirs and local postcards. When they had parked, they strolled around for a while, then went down to the beach and wandered down to the creaming waves. Louise envied the children in the swimsuits splashing in the cool water. The sun was beginning to fade, and people were packing up to go home.

They had dinner at a quiet, romantic little restaurant in a back street. Louise felt a strange sensation, seated opposite Daniel, aware that some of the female customers were eyeing him with admiring interest. In his lightweight summer suit he looked handsome, a little dangerous, somehow strange to her. She lowered her eyes, watching him through her lashes as he poured a little Moselle into her glass. He was rationing her wine, a quizzical twist to his tough mouth.

'Eat your meal,' he ordered, leaning back. 'You're just picking at it.'

Obediently she pretended to show enthusiasm about the Sole Véronique she had ordered, but she had no appetite.

'Now, tell me the truth about this art college idea,' he said. 'Is it really what you want to do?'

'I think so,' she said. 'Art is my best subject, and I must choose some sort of career.'

'You never mentioned it before,' he said. 'I thought you were just going to stay at home for a year or so.'

'I ought to train for a job,' she explained. 'You can't keep me for the rest of my life.'

'I doubt if that's likely to be necessary,' he said drily. 'I would say your future career is unlikely to require any formal training.'

She raised her eyes, the blue filled with sparkling impatience. 'Sexist! Marriage isn't a career any more.'

'No? What is it, then? How would you define it?'

'A partnership,' she said. 'I've every intention of working after I'm married.'

'How very liberated,' he said with a drawl. 'Doesn't your future husband have any say in it?'

'Not having met him, I can't say,' she shrugged.

'If I love him, he'll agree with me.'

His mouth twisted. 'Don't you mean, if he loves you?'

'No,' she said certainly. 'I wouldn't ask him to fall into line with everything I wanted just because he was in love with me.'

'What would you ask?' he enquired softly.

'Any man I chose would see things my way without having to be asked anything,' she said with confidence.

Daniel laughed shortly. 'In other words, no chauvinists need apply?'

She lifted her chin, her small oval face flushed. 'Definitely not!'

Daniel's eyes were suddenly filled with teasing laughter. 'How little you know yourself!'

She eyed him. 'What do you mean?'

'You're the most feminine creature I've ever known,' he said softly. 'There's no rebel blood in your veins, my darling.'

'You said I was changing,' she retorted.

His face sobered. 'Yes,' he said, and his eyes flashed over her, taking in the slender curved body in the seductive white dress. 'My God, yes,' he muttered, as if to himself, under his breath.

They walked back to the car side by side, barely speaking. The summer night was very warm, and the sound of the sea came like a distant whisper to their ears. Louise glanced surreptitiously at his hard profile, thinking tenderly that he looked oddly sombre, as if his thoughts were not happy.

In the car, he started the engine without a word and drove away towards Bristol very fast. She leaned back, her hands in her lap, her eyes on the dark road, wishing she understood him. For a little while that evening they had achieved the first truly equal conversation they had ever had. She had begun to feel that at last he was treating her as an adult, then she had made an incautious remark and spoilt it all.

Queen's Dower had a magical sweetness in the moonlight. The air was wine-sweet as they stood on the drive, staring up at the glittering windows, the moon turning them silver. Louise sighed pleasurably.

'Isn't it lovely to be home?' Nowhere in the world was as beautiful as Queen's Dower and she knew that if she ever had to leave it she would be an Eve shut out from the Garden of Eden for the rest of her life.

Daniel nodded. 'Yes,' he said almost curtly, turning away. She followed him into the house through the side door. They walked up the winding stone stairs to the family apartments and found that Ducky had left out a plate of wrapped sandwiches and a note ordering Louise to drink some milk before going to bed.

Teasingly, she said to him. 'At least someone still treats me as a child!'

He turned on his heel, glaring at her. 'I'll be only too happy to go on treating you as a child, Louise, but you just won't let me.'

Exquisitely submissive, swaying a little wearily in her white dress, she looked at him with huge blue eyes which were filled with drowsy regret. 'Don't, Daniel.' Her voice held a sad appeal.

His teeth snapped together. 'Oh, drink your milk and get off to bed! You look as if you're asleep on your feet.'

'All our friendly rapport seems to have evaporated suddenly,' she said in childlike resentment.

'Make up your mind whether you want to be treated as a child or as a woman,' he said coldly.

She looked at him through her lashes, a faint smile on her mouth. 'Oh? Have I got a choice?'

He caught her by the shoulders, holding her away from him. 'You're asking for trouble, and you know it, looking at me like that in that unbelievable, sexy little dress . . . from seven to seventeen in one minute, and you leave me wondering whether I'm on my head or my heels!'

'There's one certain fact in this topsy-turvy world,' she said dreamily.

'And what's that?' he asked through his teeth, staring down at her with eyes which moved restlessly over the pearly glimmer of her skin above the neckline of her dress.

'You are the very archetype of the male chauvinist,' she said, sleepily teasing.

'What a relief—out of the running, then,' he said derisively.

'Completely,' she said, her blue eyes very bright, feeling his hands tighten on her.

'You know what you're asking for, don't you?' he demanded, shaking her a little. 'Get to bed, Louise, before I give it to you.'

'You've never frightened me, Daniel,' she said sweetly, wrinkling her nose at him in a childish gesture.

'Then I damned well ought to,' he said tersely.

'I'm not Little Red Riding Hood and you aren't the Wolf,' she said, her mouth curving with laughter.

'Will you behave?' he asked grimly. 'I've never lost my temper with you yet, but I pretty soon will.'

She wanted him to kiss her so badly she was melting inside, her body seemed to be hollow and without strength. Between her lashes she surveyed his hard face longingly, the urgency of her need pushing her to tease him into coming closer.

He was staring down at her, his eyes narrowed, and she could sense that he was aware of what was happening.

'Bed,' he said curtly, 'or I swear I'll slap you.'

The tone sobered her. She stepped away and he let his hands fall from her shoulders. She got a glass of milk and turned to go, pausing to look back at him over her shoulder. 'Goodnight, Daniel. Thank you for the grown-up dinner party.' The soft thread of a taunt echoed in her voice and Daniel gave her a dark frown.

'Goodnight,' he said, his face filled with restless impatience.

In the bathroom Louise stared at her face, energetically brushing her teeth. Life, she thought, was a lot more complicated than she had imagined. A lot more exciting, too.

Coming out, barefoot and loose-haired, her face glowing with a douche of cold water, she walked straight into Daniel and stumbled. He steadied her, his glance comprehensive as it ran over the childlike pink nightdress with its sweet ruffle of white ribbon at her throat.

'Back to age ten again?' he asked sarcastically.

The blue eyes flashed defiantly at his face. 'You used to kiss me goodnight when I was ten,' she said deliberately.

'Are you hellbent on suicide?' he asked between

his teeth, then he hardened his steadying grip on her and bent his head, coolly brushing his mouth over her cheek.

'Top marks for self-control,' she told him teasingly, turning to go into her room.

He whirled her round, his face suddenly furiously angry, and clamped his arms around her, finding her mouth, forcing her head back under the driving violence of his kiss. His hands were oppressive, controlling the little flurry of resistance she gave on instinct, an incredible terrifying hardness in the way he was taking what he wanted from her. He had been angry last time, but there had been a difference ... now she felt a ruthless core of bruising force in him. Her mouth quivered, hurt and helpless under his aggression, feeling the punitive nature of the kiss, the desire to wound. For the first time in her life Daniel was deliberately hurting her, wanting to hurt her, meaning to hurt her, and she was wrenched by the realisation.

He released her with the same violence, almost throwing her away from him, faced her, breathing harshly, his face dark, his eyes leaping with bitterness.

'God, I hope that's taught you to stop playing games with me, Louise,' he said between his teeth. 'You're vulnerable, and don't forget it. I'm a damned sight stronger than you are, and if you push me too far you might get badly hurt.'

She flew into her bedroom and slammed the door. Facing it, she shouted, through coming tears, 'I hate you, Daniel ... I hate you!'

She heard his snarled reply before he stamped away. 'At least that's a sane reaction!'

She sank down on her bed, staring at herself in the mirror. Her mouth was visibly bruised, the soft pink lips slightly swollen, the eyes drowning in tears. She was trembling helplessly, incredulous as she accepted that Daniel had wanted to hurt her. All her life he had gone out of his way to please, to soothe, to comfort her . . . now he was an enemy. She threw herself down on the bed and wept.

CHAPTER THREE

SHE stayed out of Daniel's way over the next two days. He made it easy by leaving for work early and returning late, and she did not join him for their usual morning ride. When they met in the evenings she was quiet and withdrawn, leaving him to Barbara's sweet, smiling company, keeping herself well in the background.

The evening before Peter and Sally were due to arrive she was in the bathroom after Barbara had gone, washing her face and cleaning her teeth, when she heard him walking along the corridor. She had left the bathroom door open, imagining that it would be some time before he came up to bed, and hurriedly dried her face, her back to the door, hoping he would ignore her.

Instead he halted and stood there until she turned, reluctantly, her face guarded, and looked at him.

His expression was unreadable. 'How long are you going to sulk?' he asked coolly.

Her blue eyes flared. 'I am not sulking!'

'What else is it?' he asked wryly. 'You haven't exchanged a word with me for the last two days and you know it. Your guests are arriving tomorrow. If you think I'm going to be kept in the doghouse while they're here, you can think again!'

Louise walked out of the bathroom, her head in the air, a cold expression on her face, and moved towards her room.

Daniel caught her elbow, halting her. 'Answer me!'

She could not escape without a struggle, so she stood, her head averted, her body tense. 'What do you want me to say?' She deliberately used an off-hand tone.

'Don't take that tone with me!' Irritation threaded his voice now, and his hand was a vice around her slender arm.

She turned her head and looked down very coolly at the hand. 'Would you mind taking your hand off me? I can't stand having you touch me!'

There was a silence so filled with anger that it was like a thick fog between them. Daniel dropped his hand, clenching it at his side.

'That isn't the impression you've been giving me until now,' he said unpleasantly.

'I know you better than I did,' she retorted icily. 'Much better.'

'Then perhaps you'll understand this,' he said between his teeth. 'While Blare and his sister are here, you're not treating me to any more of your adolescent displays of temper. You'll kindly speak to me as politely as you do to them.'

She turned her head to face him, hauteur in her small white face, her blue eyes scornful. 'Or what?' The contemptuous drawl flicked him icily.

His face was a dark furious mask. 'Or I'll do what I should have done a long time ago, slap you silly.'

'That,' she said coldly, 'would be an improvement.'

'My God, Louise, I'm beginning to think I've totally spoilt you,' he exclaimed furiously. 'You're nothing but a little brat!'

Louise slammed her bedroom door without replying. After a moment she heard him going to his own room. She felt her body collapse, as though she had been under some tremendous strain.

She rode next morning, quite deliberately, although she did not wait for Daniel to join her. He rode up beside her ten minutes after she had left the house, and eyed her obliquely, his dark handsome face set, his white silk sweater giving him a curiously medieval look, the tight neckline emphasising the strength of his shoulders and neck, the uplift of his powerful head.

She was wearing a blue cotton shirt, open at the throat, the colour casting a faint shadow over her long white neck and the plunge between her small, high breasts. Her slender body sat gracefully on Velvet's silken back, the reins loose in her hands.

'Are we speaking again yet?' he asked her drily. 'Or am I still public enemy number one?'

She threw him a cool look. 'If I have anything to say to you I'll say it.'

'Am I supposed to grovel on my knees in gratitude?' he asked acidly.

'If I'm to be polite to you, you can be polite to me,' she retorted with an unsmiling face.

'What time is Blare getting here?' he asked, turning his horse to fall in beside her.

'Before lunch, they said,' she replied.

'Which means I shall have to be here, I suppose,' he muttered.

'Mr Blare will undoubtedly expect it,' she said, shrugging.

'Boring idiot,' he said forcefully.

'I rather like him.'

He gave her a frowning glance. 'You mean you're going to disagree with everything I say from now on, out of principle?'

Louise kicked Velvet and broke into a gallop. He came after her and passed her, hoofs thundering over the turf. She turned Velvet and rode off in the opposite direction, hearing him come after her a moment or two later. A reckless madness rose up inside her. She went straight for a holly hedge which barred her way, ignoring his sudden, hoarse cry behind her. Velvet leapt obediently, her slender legs tucked under her, and came down like a bird on the other side. Louise felt a wild rush of self-satisfaction. It was the highest fence she had ever taken, and she knew she had timed it perfectly.

The next moment Daniel was next to her, his gelding landing neatly, and she felt his hands wrench the reins out of her hand, his blue-green eyes charged with wild rage.

'My God, you little fool, you bloody nearly broke your neck.'

'Velvet took it like an angel,' she said, chin lifted defiantly, shaking back her sleek black hair.

'I ought to ...' He bit back the words, his lips tight. They stared at each other in silence.

'Well, go on, Daniel,' she said, sweetly encouraging. 'What are you going to do? Keep me on bread and water for a week? Whip me? Or far worse ... inflict one of your beastly kisses on me?'

Suddenly she realised that he was shaking, visibly shaking, his hands nerveless, and all the colour had gone from his face.

'Daniel,' she said in a husky whisper, her blue eyes contrite, 'I'm sorry.'

'Have you any idea what I went through when you took that fence?' he asked her hoarsely. 'God, I thought you could never clear it. You've never jumped that high in your life before. How could you do such a stupid thing?'

'I'm sorry, I'm sorry,' she whispered, suddenly beginning to cry.

There was a silence. She bowed her head in her hands on Velvet's silk neck, sobbing childishly. After a long pause she felt Daniel's hand on the back of her head, stroking her hair softly, but she went on crying, finding it impossible to stop, as though she were shedding tears which had been dammed up for centuries.

He stopped stroking her hair. She vaguely heard the creak of his saddle leather as he dismounted, then his hands pulled her down from Velvet's back and turned her into his arms, holding her gently, her head buried in his chest. Slowly her tears ceased. Unconsciously she sighed, her cheek turning against him, feeling the warm strength of his body under her skin.

'Better?' he asked huskily.

She nodded without speaking.

'We'd better go back to breakfast,' he said, but his arms still held her, and she made no move to get away.

For a moment they stood there while the two horses grazed, tearing at the grass, indifferent to their riders.

Then Daniel held her at arms' length, eyeing her wet face. 'You look very bedraggled,' he said teasingly. Producing a handkerchief he gently wiped her face, then flicked her hair back tenderly, his hand lingering on her forehead.

'Come on,' he said. 'I'll give you a leg up.'

Louise vaulted into the saddle and waited while he mounted too, then they rode back to the house in a harmony which approached their old easy companionship.

The Blare family arrived at noon. Their long black limousine purred up the drive and parked in front of the house. Louise ran down the steps, graceful as a ballet dancer in a lemon silk dress and fragile white shoes, flinging herself into Sally's arms with a cry of welcome.

Sally, her bronze hair shimmering in the sunlight, hugged her back. She was slightly taller than Louise, a slim girl with brown eyes like chestnuts and a broad smile filled with good humour. They had become close friends during the past year, one of those sudden relationships which occur when propinquity pushes people together who have never been very close before. Louise had known Sally for a long time, at a distance, but they had shared more interests in the past year.

Sally's father was smiling warmly as Louise turned to shake hands with him. A wealthy businessman, James Blare had made his fortune very rapidly in his middle years, and he admired and coveted the settled aura of Queen's Dower. On him Sally's bronze hair was thinner and slightly auburn, and his face bore the marks of nervous tension given by years of intense competition.

His son, Peter, was oddly fair, a tall, good-looking boy with hair the colour of corn and eyes of warm brown, like his sister.

The combination was strikingly unusual and much admired by the girls at Louise's school. Peter's open pursuit of her during the past term had only been received with favour because she felt the pressure of public opinion. Her friends expected her to be delighted by Peter's interest, and, since she had a very deep sense of privacy, she had no wish for any of them to realise how much more she preferred Daniel. They had all heard of her beloved brother, seeing him in just that light, and although she knew her own feelings had changed dramatically she had no desire to allow anyone to guess.

Daniel came out of the front door just as she was turning towards Peter, a flush on her cheeks, her eyes filled with a strange shy laughter.

'Hi,' said Peter, his voice warm. He was nearly nineteen, mature for his years because his father had long treated him as an adult and the freedom he had been given had encouraged him to think like one.

'Hi,' said Louise.

There was a peculiar pause, neither of them quite knowing whether to shake hands or not. The last time they met, at one of the school dances, Louise had let him kiss her for some time, in the shadows of the library, and the moment lay between them as they stared at each other.

Daniel said politely, 'Nice to see you again, Mr Blare.'

Louise turned to watch as the two men shook hands. Mr Blare stared up at the warm, mellow façade of the house. 'So this is Queen's Dower ... lovely, lovely ... how did it get that name? Unusual, isn't it?'

'Legend has it that the house was a gift to one of my ancestors from Queen Elizabeth for some service or other,' Daniel explained. 'The story is a little vague, but it's certain that the house has always been called that.'

'The other version is more romantic,' Louise put in.

Daniel gave her a wry, indulgent look. 'Well, go on, tell them your own version.'

'I didn't make it up!' she retorted. 'It's in a book in the library.' She smiled at Mr Blare. 'The romantic version says that the first Norfolk to live here was only eighteen when he fell in love with one of the Queen's ladies in waiting. His family wouldn't let him marry her because she had no fortune of her own, so the Queen gave her the land and the house as her dowry . . . that's much nicer, isn't it?'

'More romantic, but far less probable,' Daniel said drily.

'You have a soulless view of history,' Louise retorted, her eyes sparkling teasingly at him.

'I believe your version,' Peter said softly.

She turned and smiled at him, her smile full of warmth. 'I'm glad someone agrees with me!'

'Shall we go in to lunch?' Daniel asked coolly, shepherding his guests forward into the house. They paused, gasping with delight, to stare at the hall, then Sally ran to gaze into some of the glass cases which held family relics and began to bombard Louise with questions about them.

'I suggest Louise gives you a guided tour after lunch,' Daniel said politely. 'I'm afraid I have to drive into Bristol to my office at one-thirty so we have to have an early lunch.'

Reluctantly, Sally was dragged away from the hall

and five minutes later they were all drinking sherry and talking quiet small talk as they waited for the meal to be served.

'You promised to show me where to catch trout,' Peter said to Louise, leaning forward.

She glanced at Daniel, meeting his dry look without batting an eyelid. 'I'll be glad to,' she promised. 'They're very wily, though, and the weather is so good ... they see your shadow on the water and they're gone without a sound.'

'Then I hope the weather turns grey and gloomy,' Peter grinned.

'Don't say that!' Sally complained. 'I'm looking forward to some riding in this fabulous park.' She batted her lashes at Daniel. 'Will you allow us to ride your horses, Mr Norfolk?'

'Daniel,' he said softly, smiling into her brown eyes with a sudden display of charm which infuriated Louise.

Sally's eyes glowed. 'Daniel,' she said, as if the name were music. 'I love that name.'

'Do you?' His blue-green eyes gleamed like strange stones as he gazed into the eager face. 'Is your name really Sally, or is that short for Sarah?'

'Short for Sarah,' she agreed.

'Then may I call you that?' he asked. 'Sarah is such a musical name. It suits you.'

Sally looked as if he had kissed her, a bright radiance in her face. Louise felt a sharp knife-like pain in her stomach and was unable to hear a word of what Peter was saying to her.

'Don't you think so, Louise?' he asked suddenly.

Vaguely she blinked at him. 'Oh, yes,' she said faintly.

He beamed. 'Great.' He turned to his sister. 'Hey, Louise thinks it would be a great idea if we went dancing tonight. I told you she'd like to go.'

'Dancing?' Daniel asked, frowning. 'Where?'

'There's some sort of hotel just a few miles from here,' Peter told him. 'We saw a poster in the village as we stopped for petrol. There's a dance at the hotel tonight, and I thought Louise might like to go, and she says she would like to.'

'What hotel?' Daniel asked curtly.

'What was it called?' Peter asked his sister.

'Peacock Pie,' Sally said, giggling. 'Silly name.'

Daniel's mouth tautened. 'They get a very mixed crowd in there. I don't really think it would be suitable.'

'Why not?' Louise asked, conscious of that iron little ache in her stomach. 'I think the idea is great.'

Daniel gave her a flashing angry look. 'You've never been to one of these dances.'

'Time I found out what they were like then,' she said, lifting her chin.

Ducky came in and said the lunch was ready, and they all rose. Louise moved forward, but Daniel caught her arm, dragging her aside so that Peter and Sally followed Mr Blare, leaving them to take up the rear.

She looked at him calmly.

'You're not going,' he said between his teeth, 'and that's flat.'

She remembered the way he had smiled at Sally, his deliberate use of all his charm, and she gave him a cool glance.

'Good heavens, I'm unlikely to meet Jack the Ripper at a country dance, and after all, Peter will be there to protect me.'

He gave her a hard stare, but she gently tugged her arm out of his hold and followed their guests, leaving him no option but to come after her.

The meal was oddly muted. Mr Blare was a little uneasy with Daniel, extremely polite and eager to please him, but without any idea what to say to him. Sally was openly adoring, smiling at him with big brown eyes whenever he turned in her direction. Peter and Louise carried on a quiet, muffled conversation which died whenever there was a lull between the other three, as though they did not wish to be over-heard.

Afterwards Daniel hurtled off to Bristol with a face like thunder, and Louise showed the Blare family around the house, giving a perfect imitation of their guide, sending Sally into giggles as she told the tale of the family ghost who appeared on Easter Sunday morning as the cock crew, a Stuart man in a blue satin suit who had died at his brother's hands on Easter Sunday after finding the other man in bed with his French wife. The portrait of the French wife hung in a small saloon. Her black ringlets and bold black eyes showed well against the rich red silk she wore, and there was a wicked smile on her full mouth.

'Is this another family legend?' asked Mr Blare in amusement. 'Or is this a true story?'

'Both,' said Louise promptly, sending Sally into another fit of giggles.

'You're a tease,' scolded Mr Blare, shaking his head.

Peter looked at her out of his brown eyes, his silent gaze echoing his father's accusation, and she looked down, her eyes impudent.

Mr Blare reluctantly left after tea, and the three young people waved to him as he drove away.

Sally sighed rapturously. 'A whole fortnight of this!' Her eyes ran delightedly over the shady green park and the red brick of the house. 'And Daniel, too! You never told me he was so fantastic ... a dream, sexy and tough, but charming with it. Imagine having a brother like that!' She gave Peter a taunting smile. 'And I had to get stuck with him!'

'Isn't she just sweet?' Peter said scathingly. 'What luck to have her for a sister!'

'Shall I show you the trout stream?' Louise asked, to divert their attention from the squabble which was shaping. She knew how they could boil over with rage in one of their rows, even though they were basically attached to each other.

'Fantastic,' Peter agreed, taking her hand.

They walked along, linked, while Sally sauntered after them, making pointed little remarks about young love. The swift-running trout stream flowed through the far boundary of the park. A millstream at one point, it had a rapid pace, and was well stocked with trout. They strolled along the green banks watching the speckled fish hovering just below a slight dam which sent the water toppling down a slope. 'This is the best place,' Louise told them. 'They wait here to take food as it comes over the dam. It isn't very sporting to take them here, but it always works.'

Their shadows disturbed the fish who vanished into green weed. Peter watched, fascinated, as they reappeared later. Deep in the woods they heard the cooing of the wood pigeons. One fluttered near them, soft grey, startled, with bright beady eyes, and Sally sighed deeply.

'Oh, this is the most fabulous place, Louise. It must have been hell to leave it to go to school.'

'I hated leaving,' Louise said with all honesty.

They sat down on the grass in the park, stretching out in the afternoon sunshine, enjoying the warm silence which surrounded them.

'Heaven,' sighed Sally. 'Sheer heaven!'

'Yes,' Peter murmured, leaning on one elbow to look into Louise's exquisite oval face.

She felt herself blushing, and looked away. Sally grew restless after a moment or two and got up. 'I'm going to take a look at your sheep,' she said. 'Funny animals, sheep. Funny eyes they've got. They don't bite, do they?'

Louise laughed. 'Not unless you bite them first.'

Sally looked startled.

'I'm teasing,' Louise said. 'No, they don't bite. They're very timid.'

Sally wandered off and Louise lay on her back staring up into the deep blue sky, her hands beneath her head, conscious of Peter's long stare.

'Your eyes are exactly the colour of that sky,' he said in a conversational tone.

'How nice,' she said, giving him a little sideways smile.

'And your hair is as black as that raven's feathers,' he added, waving a hand towards the male of a pair of ravens who were lurching along the grass in their ungainly fashion.

'Ravens always remind me of Richard the Third,' she said.

Peter looked blank, taken aback, cut off in the middle of his rehearsed string of compliments.

'Haven't you ever noticed the way they waddle

along like hunchbacks?' she asked him. 'Very dignified but comic.'

Peter looked cross for a moment, then suddenly bent over her smiling face and kissed her mouth clumsily, holding her shoulders down against the grass.

Louise made no attempt to struggle, accepting the kiss without either resistance or enthusiasm.

Peter looked down at her, very flushed. 'You're the most beautiful girl I've ever seen,' he said huskily. 'I'm crazy about you.'

She blushed then, her lashes falling. The real emotion in his voice had thrown her off balance, and the game had suddenly turned serious.

Before she could reply Sally came back, laughing. 'I've just seen the most adorable lamb with cross eyes ... he skipped about and looked horrified whenever I went near him ...'

Louise got up, smoothing down her crumpled skirt, brushing the grass off it with a shaky hand. 'We might as well walk back to the house. Daniel will be home soon.'

Sally linked arms with her, whispering, 'Darling angel pie, do ask Daniel to come to the dance tonight ... if he doesn't come, I shan't have a partner, and after all, if he isn't keen on you going to it alone, he ought to be there to make sure you're safe.'

Louise gave her a wry look. 'You ask him,' she said. 'I'm not going to.'

'Don't be such a spoilsport,' Sally protested, brown eyes disgusted. 'I can't ask him.'

'Well, I'm not asking him for any favours,' Louise said, her mouth firm.

'I thought you and Daniel got on like a house on

fire,' Sally said in surprise.

'He's a bully,' Louise said crossly. 'If you want him to come, you ask him.'

Sally did, over dinner, her prettty face pleading unashamedly, and Daniel glanced across the table at Louise, who pretended to be concentrating on her plate.

'If you don't come we'll be a threesome,' Sally begged, brown eyes wide. 'And I'll be playing gooseberry.'

'We can't have that, can we?' Daniel asked drily. 'Very well, Sarah, I'll be happy to escort you to the dance. At least I can make sure the three of you come to no harm.'

Peter looked up, offended. 'I'd make sure of that,' he said, his square chin aggressive.

Daniel gave him a cool, wry smile. 'I'm sure you would,' he said, his tone implying the opposite.

After dinner they all went up to change. Louise took down the prettiest dress she had bought on her shopping spree in Bristol, a fragile silky straight slip of deep blue which echoed her eyes. When she was dressed she surveyed herself with deep satisfaction. In the shop she had felt sure it would suit her, but now, studying herself at her leisure, she knew she had never worn anything that looked as well on her. The fine material clung everywhere, moulding her slender body like a glove. Her shoulders were naked except for two thin strips of blue which held up the dress.

Despite this the neckline was very modest, cutting across her chest in a straight line. The dress fell to below her knees, and the blue silk shimmered when she moved, outlining every inch of her with a flame-like brightness.

She brushed her hair until it shone and fastened it high on her head with a long silver slide so that it fell in a curled tail to her shoulders. Carefully she took out the make-up she had bought secretly. Until today she had never used it, but her eyes were secretive as she stared back at her reflection, softly outlining her mouth in a pale pink, just dusting her eyelids with blue.

Adding a final touch of a floral perfume at wrists and ears, she looked at herself triumphantly.

The schoolgirl who had got off the train only a few days ago might never have existed. The mirror showed her a slender, seductive young creature whose graceful movements shimmered in the light.

She went out and wandered into the sitting-room. Daniel was leaning on the window, staring out into the park with his back to her. He had put on a dark suit and white shirt, and looked older, more formal than usual.

Turning, he glanced towards her, then froze. Louise stood demurely while his opalescent eyes slowly took in every delectable inch from her shining black hair to her small feet.

The eyes came back to her face, narrowed in hard, unsmiling speculation. 'Congratulations,' he said tightly. 'This, I take it, is the final transformation . . . chrysalis into butterfly.'

'How do I look?' she asked sweetly, blue eyes innocent.

'Damnably seductive, as if you didn't know,' he said.

'You don't approve?' Her smile was mock soothing.

'No, I don't damned well approve,' he snapped. 'From schoolgirl into siren in one stage is a bit too fast.'

'This is a fast world,' she said sweetly. 'Men have been to the moon.'

'You may find yourself there if you're not careful,' he threatened.

'Not alone, I hope,' she said, and began to laugh.

He moved towards her, menace in his face, but Sally came into the room, a little shy, flushed and excited. Daniel stopped short and looked at her, producing a charming smile like a conjuror producing a rabbit from a hat.

Sally was wearing an orange trouser suit in a material as silky as the one Louise wore. She looked startling, dramatic, extremely chic, and the two girls gave each other appraising, admiring pleased looks.

'You look delightful, Sarah,' said Daniel, moving up to her, his glittering eyes smiling into her flushed face. 'I can see I shall have to fight off rivals all evening!'

Peter joined them a moment later and they set off, Daniel and Sally walking first, while the other two brought up the rear. Daniel helped Sally into the passenger seat and turned to watch as Peter, with exaggerated attention, helped Louise into the back.

The drive only took a few moments. The car park of the Peacock Pie was already crowded with cars. The music came loudly from the main room which, during the weekday, doubled as a dining-room, only converting at night to a ballroom for the midweek and weekend dances.

They found a table in a corner and sat down, attracting some attention, since everyone for miles around knew Daniel at least by sight. The manager of the hotel came up to speak to him, delighted by his presence, and while they talked, Peter led Louise on to the floor. At the moment most of the dancers were young. Some of them were dancing apart, some were dancing close to each other, their arms around each other's necks, moving with slow steps.

Louise hesitated, uncertain. Peter grinned, taking her hands and placing them round his neck, his own arms encircling her waist.

They moved in imitation of the other dancers, and Louise felt a flush growing on her cheeks, aware of Daniel's stare from the other side of the room. Peter pulled her closer, looking down into her face.

'I've been waiting for a chance to tell you how fabulous you look,' he whispered. 'You're magic ... absolutely magic, Louise. That's the sexiest dress I've even seen, and on you it looks fantastic.'

Her blue eyes danced. 'Thank you,' she smiled. 'You'll turn my head with all these compliments!'

'I mean every word,' he said earnestly, his brown eyes filled with admiration. 'Even in your school uniform you were lovely, but in this you're breathtaking.'

She gave him a slow, charming smile, her lashes fluttering. 'You'll make me blush!'

He grinned. 'You are blushing,' he said.

The music ended and they returned to the table, hand in hand. Daniel stared pointedly at their linked hands and Peter, a little pink, released her as he sat down. Sally was drinking a glass of champagne, giggling as the bubbles got caught in her nose.

Daniel poured a glass for Peter, then half filled one for Louise, who looked at him in irritation.

'I can drink a whole glass, you know,' she said. 'I'm the same age as Sally.'

'You aren't used to it,' he said flatly. 'Sarah tells me she's often drunk a glass of champagne.'

Louise held out her glass in silence.

He eyed her grimly. 'You can have some later,' he said.

Crossly she drank the champagne very quickly, ignoring the narrowed look of his blue-green eyes, then held out her glass again, staring at him with a lifted chin.

Daniel's mouth set. He silently refilled her glass, this time right to the top, meeting her blue gaze with a cold stare.

She sipped it, this time, then Peter stood up, saying, 'Excuse us, won't you?' Louise put down her glass and followed him on to the floor, her slender body slipping sensuously into his arms. The champagne had given her a deeper flush, a singing rhythm in her limbs. She moved gracefully in Peter's arms, his hands on her waist, her chin on his shoulder.

The evening wore on delightedly. She danced every dance with Peter, her blue eyes very bright, her skin with the peach-like flush of excitement the champagne had engendered.

Sally and Daniel had danced a number of times, too, but Daniel had introduced Sally to a couple of young men whom he knew, and once or twice Louise saw her dancing with one of them while Daniel wandered around talking to other guests whom he knew.

It was towards the end of the evening that Daniel

intercepted her before Peter could lead her on to the floor yet again.

'My dance this time, I think,' he said coolly, taking her wrist.

Peter fell back politely and returned to the table. Louise felt her heart thudding with abrupt violence against her breast. Daniel looked down at her, totally expressionless. 'This is the way you dance, isn't it?' he asked her as if she were a stranger, and took her hands and lifted them around his neck, his own hands pulling her close against his body.

They began to move in total harmony, their bodies so close she could hear the beating of his heart, feel each movement of his thighs as he guided her around the floor.

The lights suddenly went low. 'Last waltz,' the master of ceremonies whispered through the microphone, and the music softened to a dreamy sweetness.

Louise was almost stunned by the sensations which were rushing through her. Daniel was holding her so close she could barely move without brushing against the whole length of his body.

His hands slid slowly, caressingly over her back and hips and her eyes closed involuntarily, her face against his hard shoulder, her fingertips very cautiously ruffling his dark hair, finding the strong muscles of his neck.

Heat was burning in the centre of her body. She was trembling, aware that if he let her go she might well fall to the ground, her knees so weak they might have been made of jelly.

Daniel turned his head and she felt his mouth softly touch her ear, slide down her throat and over her shoulder. She gave a stifled little whimper of pleasure, clinging to him.

'Siren,' he whispered, his lips at her ear.

She was incapable of answer, of movement, so intensely aware of him that she was in delirium.

The lights came up slowly, the music died away. Daniel detached her as if she were a limpet clinging to a rock, and looked down into her wildly flushed, brilliant-eyed little face.

His mouth was hard with amusement. She looked up at him, standing still, trembling, unable to disguise exactly what effect he had had on her.

'You're out of your league, sweetheart,' he said softly, a barbed taunt in his voice. 'Stick with your toys for a few more years.'

Louise drew herself up, her flush abating, then turning she walked over to the table. Peter stared at her oddly, his eyes jealous, and she gave him a radiant smile.

'I'm stifling in here,' she said softly. 'Shall we walk outside in the fresh air for a few minutes before we go home? I'm so hot!'

When Daniel came to the table two moments later he found Sally there alone, a conspiratorial grin on her pretty face. He glanced around, not having seen Louise and Peter leave.

'Where are the other two? It's time we went, I think.'

'They've gone for a midnight stroll around the car park,' Sally said, her eyes dancing. 'Peter was feeling distinctly romantic. That dress of Louise's has had a damaging effect on his heart.'

Daniel was not amused. He lifted her to her feet.

'We'll find them and get home,' he said crisply. 'I have to go to work in the morning even if you three don't.'

Out in the car park Louise and Peter stood in the shadows. She lifted her face to him and Peter eagerly kissed her, his mouth pleasantly warm and adoring. She heard Daniel's footsteps approaching, and lifted her arms around Peter's neck, swaying against him. Peter groaned and tightened his hold on her, suddenly kissing her very hard. It was not an unpleasant sensation. Her dance with Daniel, the champagne, the heat, had made her drowsily receptive. She kissed him back softly, her head tilted back.

'We're going,' said Daniel from a few feet away, the harsh bite of his voice only just stopping short of open rage.

Peter jumped away, surprised. He had not heard anyone coming. Louise gracefully moved past him, her blue dress shimmering in the light, her dark head high, averted from Daniel.

He seized her arm in a grip that bit into her flesh, and pushed her forcefully into the passenger seat at the front of the car. Sally, looking sleepy, was bundled into the back beside her brother, and the car shot out of the car park at a rate which made Louise snap awake. Daniel drove, staring straight ahead, his profile taut.

During the short drive home not a word was said. Sally was almost asleep. Peter was dazed, dreamy, after the exchange of kisses.

Louise glanced under her lashes at Daniel's hard face as she said goodnight to him. Their guests wandered off to their rooms, yawning. Daniel caught her wrist and pushed her into her bedroom, advancing towards her with a grim expression.

'You are still my ward, Louise,' he said between his straight, hard lips. 'So listen to me very closely ... you're not just growing up, you're accelerating like a rocket, and it must stop. Young Blare will lose his head if you give him any more green lights. You're playing with dynamite and you know it. Ease off or I'll send him packing, and I'm not joking.'

She looked at him coolly. 'Yes, Daniel. Certainly, Daniel. Three bags full, Daniel.'

His eyes blazed. 'That can stop, too. You're not stampeding me into making a fool of myself, again, Louise. Just play it cool with the boy. He's at the emotional stage where he might get out of hand, and you're not up to handling that situation.'

She was suddenly tired, emotionally exhausted. She turned away, yawning. 'Goodnight, Daniel.'

'I'm totally serious,' he said forcefully. 'Do you hear me, Louise?'

'I should think they can hear you in the village,' she said, her eyes defiant.

'If you want to have those two here for two weeks, you'll do as I say,' he snapped.

'Oh, very well,' she said, sitting down abruptly. 'Go away. I've got a headache.'

'Serves you right,' he said callously. 'I told you to lay off the champagne, or is it the kisses that have gone to your head?'

She looked at him through her lashes, her face wearing a secretive sensual smile. 'Both, probably.'

He stared at her, his eyes restless. 'One of these days I'll go completely crazy and teach you a lesson you'll never forget,' he said.

'I thought you already had,' she said sweetly.

Daniel turned on his heel and slammed out of the room.

CHAPTER FOUR

IN the morning, Daniel had gone to work when Louise got up, and she spent the day in a peaceful, leisurely fashion with her two guests, riding, sunbathing, walking in the park. The summer weather continued golden and unchanging, the faint south wind blowing just enough to halt the upward climb of the temperature and make the sun bearable. Sally was ecstatic as, in a yellow bikini, she lounged in the garden on a low chair, her skin smoothly oiled, her eyes shielded by sunglasses. 'This is the very nicest way of spending time I've ever discovered,' she said. 'If I lived here I would never want to leave the park gates.'

Louise was feeling faintly conspicuous as she lay beside her friend. The plain black swimsuit she had always worn at school had been pronounced with a shriek of gleeful horror as unwearable, and Sally had insisted, despite her reluctance, on lending her the spare bikini she had brought with her. A coral colour, alarmingly diminutive, it had made her feel quite naked as she came out of the house wearing it, feeling Ducky's appalled gaze on her as she went past. Nothing had been said, but Louise had known what was going on inside Ducky's round, bullet head.

Peter in blue and white trunks lay on the lawn eyeing her from the safety of his sunglasses, but she pretended to be unaware of his admiring stare. After last night she felt like playing safe. Daniel had had a distinctly menacing air after the dance.

Through the warm summer air the sound of a car travelled to them. Louise did not move, her nerves tightening in anticipation, but Sally sat up eagerly. 'Daniel's coming back,' she said.

'He can't be,' said Louise, pretending to yawn. 'It's only five o'clock. He gets back at six.'

'Visitors, then,' said Peter, a little crossly. Louise had held him at arms' length all day, and he was beginning to sulk.

Daniel came round the corner of the house, Barbara walking beside him, and surveyed the scene on the smooth green lawn with a raised eyebrow. Louise did not move, even when he took his time to inspect the curved length of her body in the coral bikini. The enormous coloured sunglasses she wore protected her expression from him.

'You all look as if you're having a good time,' Barbara commented, laughing in an amused way. Her dark eyes shot towards Peter, taking in his youth and good looks, and her smile widened.

'Barbara, this is Sally Blare and her brother Peter,' Daniel introduced quietly. 'Sally and Peter, this is Barbara.'

Peter took off his sunglasses to smile at her, his brown eyes admiring. In the slim green dress and very high heels, Barbara's sophistication was outstanding. Her exquisitely applied cosmetics, her air of self-confidence, her smouldering dark eyes, gave her a mysterious aura which was more valuable than beauty.

'It's so warm,' Barbara said, looking around. 'I'm dying for a long, cool drink.'

Louise slid off the lounger and stood up, her dark

head held high. 'I'll go and get some for all of us,' she offered politely. 'Have my chair, Barbara.'

Barbara gave her a brief smile. 'Thank you.' She sank down gracefully, sighing as she stretched out. 'While you three have been sunning yourselves all day I've been working in the shop.'

'You work in a shop?' Peter sounded curious.

'I have an antique shop,' Barbara smiled at him sideways, her lashes fluttering. Artificial lashes, Louise thought scornfully. No woman in the world ever had lashes that thick, that long, that black. She walked towards the house, her bare feet stinging from the heat of the paved path.

In the empty kitchen she bent over the refrigerator, getting out the tray of ice cubes and a tall green jug of home-made lemonade which Ducky had put in there to chill some hours earlier. She stood on the kitchen stool, her slender body stretching, reaching into an upper cupboard to fetch down the glasses which matched the jug. The stool rocked and she gave a cry of alarm, but before she had time to over-balance she felt strong hands steadying her, and looked down, seeing Daniel's face at an odd angle, his opalescent eyes shimmering up at her.

She said huskily, 'Thank you.'

The touch of his cool fingers on her warm skin was deeply pleasant. She handed down the glasses and he placed them on the kitchen table, then his hands encircled her waist, lifting her down as lightly as if she were still a child. He took his time in releasing her, and she kept her eyes down, so conscious of him that her heart was hammering.

'Is this another of your Bristol purchases?' he asked drily, flipping a lazy finger towards the bikini.

'No, Sally lent it to me.'

'Ah. She's a precocious child.'

'Mature for her years?' Her tone carried a sting.

'More mature than some,' he retorted.

'Then she'll have a lot to teach me,' she said, refusing to be hurt by the remark.

His hands tightened on her waist. 'You'll learn what I want you to learn.'

Louise slowly lifted her eyes, her lashes leaving the brilliant blue eyes free and dazzling. 'I'm learning all the time,' she said softly.

'Yes,' he said grimly, 'you are, damn you.'

'Don't you like the bikini?' she asked, her slender body very pliant and submissive in his hands.

His eyes flicked over it and a wry grimace twisted his mouth. 'You know you look sensational in it,' he said flatly. 'Peter has no doubt been telling you so ever since he set eyes on it.'

She giggled, suddenly ten years old, her eyes dancing. 'Magic, he said, pure magic—it's his favourite word at the moment.'

'And you know all about magic,' Daniel drawled sardonically. 'It's in the blood, isn't it? Every female child has it in her pram, flirting and fluttering her eyes at every male who looks at her.'

'Did I?' Louise opened her eyes very wide, pushing back the long black hair with one hand.

'You were exquisite as a child,' he said, almost sombrely. 'Like Snow White, all black hair, white skin and great blue eyes ... a walking dream.'

She suddenly grew solemn. 'I was terrified of that story, do you remember?'

'You took it personally,' he said, his mouth tender. 'The witch, the dark forest, the animals ... they were all very real to you. You always had an over-sensitive, over-imaginative reaction to everything.'

She lowered her eyes, a flush in her cheeks. Even to you, Daniel? she thought sadly. Is that the truth? Did I imagine your response to me because I wanted it so badly?

Turning away, she arranged the drink, the glasses, the ice cubes on a tray and Daniel carried it out to the garden. It was greeted with wild enthusiasm. Louise lay down on the grass, refusing to take back her chair from Barbara, stretching out beside Peter, her slender body relaxed in the sunshine, the coral bikini a splash of bright colour against her pale brown limbs. Daniel sat down beside Barbara's lounger, leaning back on his hands, his eyes behind his dark lashes running slowly over the seductive slight body in coral. Peter turned on his elbow to look down at her, and his eyes were eagerly admiring.

'What shall we do tonight?' he asked.

'Have dinner, play cards,' she suggested. 'Something quiet and peaceful ... I'm exhausted by all this pleasure-seeking.' And her blue eyes teased him with laughter in their depths.

'You've got a record player,' he said. 'We could dance again.' He glanced politely at Daniel. 'If you've no objections, sir?'

Daniel's face was unreadable. 'I've no reason to object,' he said coolly.

'It sounds a very pleasant way of passing the evening,' Louise said softly.

'I agree,' Barbara chimed in, her glance at Daniel inviting.

Sally's face was flushed, her mouth turned down at the edges. Louise saw the jealous frown on her face and felt a touch of compassion for her friend. She should have warned her that Daniel was not exactly free and unattached, but then she had been so busy in resenting Daniel's charming attentions to Sally last night that she had not thought to say anything to her friend about it. Lying back, her eyes closed, she felt a resentful shiver run down her back. Adolescents, she thought gloomily. That was what they both were, and there, in her stylish elegant green dress, lay Barbara, the woman ... real woman, experienced, confident, bright with the gloss of knowledge.

Dinner that evening was an over-bright affair. Sally had wit enough to cover her jealous irritation as Barbara dominated Daniel's attention as far as she could, her scarlet talons on his arm, her dark eyes riveted on his face. Louise, in her turn, used Peter as her shield, smiling brilliantly at him, her small, oval face exquisite in the lamplight, laughing at all his jokes very softly, listening as if he fascinated her, and never once looking towards Daniel.

Barbara noticed. Her dark eyes were shrewdly amused as she looked at the two young people from time to time, seeing Peter's glazed, adoring emotions as he concentrated on Louise.

'Where's the little schoolgirl gone?' she asked Daniel very softly under cover of their laughter. 'Amazing what first love will do, isn't it? She's beginning to look almost grown up. That boy is head over heels, isn't he?'

Daniel's sardonic face did not alter. The blue-green flash of his eyes slipped like a dart of lightning over Louise once, then was quickly withdrawn. 'It happens to us all,' he drawled.

'You, too?' Barbara asked teasingly.

He gave her a wry smile. 'I was eighteen once.'

'Difficult to imagine,' Barbara flattered, her eyes travelling over the dark strength of his face, the lean hard body.

'True, all the same.'

'Were you as madly in love as Peter?' Barbara asked, smiling.

Daniel flicked a look at the boy, his eyes gleaming between their dark lashes. 'Who knows? At that age you think it's love when it's often only wish-fulfilment.'

'And was she as pretty as Louise?' Barbara asked, knowing she was oddly jealous of his little sister, although it was absurd.

Louise had heard every word, under cover of listening to Peter, had caught the nuances of the two soft voices, had comprehended Barbara's dislike of her, the faintly breathed hostility whenever that silvery voice spoke her name.

She waited urgently to hear Daniel reply. He was a long time in answering.

'She was a ravishing blonde,' he said lightly at last. 'Expensive, alluring and totally selfish. I fell out of love as quickly as I fell in—which is the best way to do it. Love is a delicious illness one should contract as rarely as possible.'

'Oh, a cynic,' said Barbara, laughing, yet with an undertone of hardness. 'So you're inoculated against love, Daniel?'

His voice was amused, crisp. 'I had my injections, but who knows if they really took?'

Louise allowed herself the luxury of glancing at him, under cover of her dark lashes, and found his eyes on her, their gleam curiously hard.

She looked quickly away, smiling at Peter. She really liked Peter, she told herself. He was fun to be with, and his admiration was balm to her soul.

After dinner Peter enthusiastically cleared a space in the sitting-room, chose a pile of records and carefully arranged them in order on the turntable. As the first one began to spin he held out his hands to Louise, who swayed submissively into his arms. Barbara and Daniel were drinking brandy in the dining-room still. Sulkily Sally lounged on a chair, her feet under her, watching as her brother and Louise moved round the room.

Louise was aware of Daniel's entry even though she had her eyes closed, her cheek against Peter's shoulder. The wild leap of her pulses warned her before Daniel spoke.

'Do you want to dance, Sally?'

Sally was on her feet, eager and smiling, her gloomy mood having evaporated. Louise realised that Barbara must have gone, after all, and wondered why. Had Daniel suggested it? It would have been awkward for him to share his attention between Sally and the older woman, and Barbara was not likely to sit idly by and watch him devote his charming smiles to the girl all evening.

Peter had turned down all the lights except the one lamp beside his sister's chair. The room was romantic, the music a whispering thread as the two couples softly swayed around, avoiding each other.

Peter's records dropped one after another, and both he and Louise tirelessly danced each one, moving softly in each other's arms, not talking. Daniel broke off his third dance with Sally to go and get a drink for both of them. His curt question to Peter was given a silent negative, a smiling shake of the head before the boy turned back towards Louise.

'I'm beginning to feel giddy,' Louise murmured into Peter's ear after a while.

He grinned at her. 'Good,' he said teasingly.

She laughed, her eyes flirtatious. 'Beast!'

'If you fall, I'll catch you,' he promised.

Her blue eyes danced. 'I'm terrified!'

Close to her ear, he murmured. 'I wish your brother would shove off. He cramps my style.'

'What style is that?' she mocked.

'If he went, I'd show you,' Peter said darkly.

Her laughter was infectious. He laughed back at her, but his eyes held excitement.

'Magic Louise,' he murmured, just as one record died away and the machinery dropped down another. His whisper reached Daniel and as Louise glanced towards him she caught the watchful hardness of his eyes on her. She looked away again quickly, aware that he was angry.

When the next record ended, he appeared beside them, his face bland. 'Time for a change of partners,' he said with a cool smile. 'Dance with your sister, Peter.'

Sulkily, Peter relinquished Louise to him, and went off to grab Sally from her chair.

'Have I got to?' she asked plaintively. 'This cave-man stuff isn't my line, brother dear.'

'Shut up and dance,' muttered Peter, his mouth resentful.

Louise was dancing with Daniel stiffly, her body held away from him, unwilling to permit a repeat performance of what had happened last time, although she was aching inwardly to feel his body pressed against her.

He looked down at her, his lids half lowered. 'Why are you dancing like a wooden jointed doll? That wasn't how you danced with him.'

She let her blue eyes drift coldly over his face. 'He's my boy-friend,' she said pointedly.

Daniel smiled, mockery in his eyes. 'Oh, is that the reason? I thought it might be something else.'

'Big brother, your imagination is playing tricks on you,' she said sweetly.

His hand jerked her violently forward and their bodies met with an impact that brought a soft, smothered gasp of pleasure out of her. He looked down at her, his face cruel. Louise was burning with anger. He knew what that contact was doing to her and he was deliberately inflicting it, as he had deliberately hurt her when he kissed her.

He was right, she thought; the abyss of time between them was too great. He had the experience to know exactly how she felt while she was incapable of reading his thoughts, except when the depth of his feelings permitted her to catch a glimpse of what was going on under his hard surface.

The relationship was too unequal. It would only lead to bitter pain for her, and the destruction of their old alliance.

'I'm tired,' she said, pretending to yawn. 'I think I'll go to bed now.'

Daniel halted, dropping his arms away from her, watching her out of his blue-green eyes.

Peter and Sally halted too. Peter protested, 'It's early yet.'

'Eleven,' Daniel said curtly. 'Louise isn't used to

late hours, remember. We were all up very late last night. I think we should call it a day for now.'

Reluctantly, Peter had to agree. Louise drifted off to bed, feeling tired and miserable, and lay in the darkness wondering how she was going to fight her way out of the emotional tangle she had found herself in without losing any of her self-respect.

The following day was a Saturday. Bright, clear and golden, it hung over the park like a luminous cloud, gilding the windows and making the shade under the trees doubly inviting. Daniel suggested a drive to the sea.

'Perfect weather for swimming,' Sally beamed, relieved to discover he had not invited Barbara.

They took a picnic with them, cold game pie and salad, fruit and cheese.

The visit to the sea was a great success. They drove to a quiet little bay which Daniel knew just outside Weston. To reach the sands they had to climb up a wooded slope and down the cliffs on the other side, but the long trail was well worth the effort. Below them as they halted on the green turf of the cliff they saw the pale yellow sands, the blue water, the waves foaming in to the beach. There was not another human being in sight; the difficulties of reaching the little cove made it an unpopular spot for families with small children.

Louise was wearing her white dress over her borrowed bikini. She knelt on the sand, unzipping it, and felt Daniel coolly remove the dress, his hands lingering on her bare shoulders. Her nerves tingled, but she gave him a polite smile of gratitude, then ran down to the sea with Peter and splashed into the waves, shrieking like a child at the coldness of the water as it hit her warm body.

She and Peter swam lazily, striking out from the shore, then drifting back again. Sally and Daniel joined them, and Louise gave him a quick, all-seeing look, her heart thudding at the hard masculinity of the lean body in black trunks.

Sally and Daniel floated, their fingers joined, playing a childish game, Sally's laughter making Louise grit her teeth with jealous resentment. Peter dived neatly, his long legs coiled, and swam beneath his sister, suddenly pulling her down into the water in a boisterous impulse which made her scream and kick away from him.

'Enjoying yourself?' Daniel asked, his head appearing beside Louise.

The mockery in his tone brought sick misery into her throat. She turned without a word and struck out for the open sea, swimming strongly, her slender body sliding through the blue water. The sun was hot on her wet body. The gulls screaming around the cliffs dived down into the waves a few feet away and bobbed like ducks, their cruel beaks striking down into the water. She swam without thinking, feeling the emotions churning around inside her, then halted, realising how far she was getting from the shore, and turned to swim back.

It was at that moment that cramp struck. The sudden shooting agony doubled her up, making her halt with a groan. She felt salt water lurch into her open mouth, spat it out with distaste, fear making her tense. Every time she tried to swim the cramp seemed worse. Panic rose inside her and she tried to lift her head to look for Daniel, instinct making her turn towards him for help.

Through the haze of pain, fear and growing alarm she heard his voice call her urgently. She lifted an arm, helpless as a child, calling him.

'Cramp ...' she groaned, swimming slowly towards where his voice had come from, each movement an agony.

It seemed endless minutes passed before his arms came round her, turning her on to her back, towing her towards the beach at a remorseless rate. He walked up the beach, pulling her dead weight after him, and laid her on the sand. Peter and Sally ran after them, watching in anxiety as Daniel bent over her.

'I'm sorry,' she gasped, her muscles still locked cruelly. 'I didn't realise how far I'd gone ...'

Daniel was white, blindingly angry, his eyes biting into her face. 'You stupid little fool!' he snapped. 'You might have drowned! How many times have I told you never to swim out like that alone?'

Tears rose in her eyes. 'I'm sorry,' she sobbed.

'She didn't mean to do it,' Peter said accusingly, glaring at Daniel. 'Don't shout at her.'

'She needs to be shouted at,' Daniel snapped. 'She deserves to be slapped hard for what she just did.'

'Well, don't you try it,' Peter retorted, flushed and aggressive, his eyes very belligerent.

Daniel surveyed him with narrowed, contemptuous eyes and rose, a very tall, very powerful man, his wide shoulders and lean hips giving him a look of awe-inspiring authority. The younger man faced him, his fair-skinned face very red, bristling jealously, protectively.

There was a tense silence, and Louise felt alarm in her throat. She impulsively put out a hand and curled it round Daniel's bare ankle, holding him, afraid he might hit Peter. There was no doubt in anyone's mind that Peter had no chance against him. It took courage for the boy even to attempt to outface him.

Daniel looked down at her and the wet blue eyes pleadingly met his gaze, and his jaw clenched. He pulled his foot out of her grasp and walked away. Peter knelt down and tentatively patted her salt-bloomed shoulder.

'Feeling better, darling?' The tender tone made her burst into scalding tears.

Daniel was laying out the white cloth on which they would eat their picnic. Sally began to unpack the food. Daniel's blue-green eyes icily watched as Peter clumsily lifted Louise's slender body into his arms, stroking her hair as she wept against him. The almost naked weight of her slight body sent a wave of hot colour to Peter's hairline. His face was easy to read as he hesitantly ran his hand down from the saturated black hair to the pale gold silk of the bare back. Louise, crying weakly, felt it herself and was suddenly alarmed. Peter's fingers were trembling with desire and excitement as she lay so close to his bare skin, the seductive curves of her body abandoned to his hands.

She pulled herself together and sat away from him, drying her moist face with her hands in a childish gesture. Through her fingers she saw Daniel staring hard at her.

She smiled carefully at Peter. 'Thank you,' she whispered, and he gave her an eager, ardent smile.

She sat brushing her tangled hair free of salt,

squatting on her heels, ignoring the preparations the other two were making. The sun burnt down, drying her bikini and her damp body, leaving the faint salty encrustation of the sea on her skin. She was wearing no make-up. Her oval face was sun-flushed and delicately tinted with a growing tan. Her mouth, innocent of lipstick, had a pink pallor which was entirely becoming, innocently alluring.

'Come and get it,' Sally shouted. 'Break up the love talk, you two. Even Romeo and Juliet had to eat!'

Louise laughed, turning her head, the wet black strands brushing her shoulder, to give Peter her hand so that he could lift her to her feet. She winced as her cramped muscles moved, and he slid an arm around her small waist, helping her towards the picnic cloth.

Daniel was lying on his side, watching them from beneath dark brows. Sally giggled, teasing her brother. 'Can't you take your hands off her even for one minute?'

Louise sat down gracefully and allowed Peter to pile a collection of food on to a plate for her. He waited on her assiduously throughout the meal, watching her with such glowing eyes that she felt her own cheeks sting with colour under them.

She avoided Daniel's gaze, conscious of it all the time. After lunch they cleared the things away, neatly returning everything to the straw hamper Ducky had packed for them, then they spread out on the sands and relaxed for an hour in the burning sun. A few other energetic souls clambered down the cliff behind them and wandered along the sands, talking, but then they vanished up the other side of the cliff and went on further, leaving the little cove deserted apart from the four lying on the beach.

'It's too hot,' said Peter, getting up, too young, too restless to lie still for long. 'Coming into the sea again, Louise?'

She sleepily raised her head, the long black hair gleaming in the sun.

'No!' Daniel said forcefully.

Peter gave him a resentful glare, but dared not argue. Sally got up and followed him down the beach. They dived into the sea like seals and swam out into the blue waters.

Alone with Daniel, Louise felt her heartbeat quicken until it almost deafened her. She lay on her stomach, her fingers restlessly filtering the fine sand, aware of him a few feet away.

He moved suddenly, rolling nearer, and she turned her head in quick alarm to find him so close their arms could touch.

He surveyed her smoulderingly. 'So how does it feel?' he asked bitingly.

She opened her eyes wide, innocent. 'What?'

'Being taught how to feel like a woman,' he said between his teeth.

Her skin slowly flushed a deep rose pink. She turned her head away and didn't answer.

'If you're not careful, the boy will lose his head over you,' Daniel said harshly. 'He's already on the verge of it. Keep him at arms' length unless you want a rather more intimate and irreversible lesson, Louise.'

'Oh!' she gasped softly, shocked and resentful. 'Peter wouldn't ...' Her words broke off in wild embarrassment, preferring not to finish that sentence.

'Wouldn't he?' Daniel's voice was scalding. 'Is that a bet?'

She made no answer, staring down at the fine glinting silvery sand her fingers were playing with.

'He wants you,' Daniel said suddenly, very close, very clipped.

The colour was flooding up her throat now and she was trembling. 'Go away!' she muttered wildly.

'What's the matter? Did you think all it amounted to was holding hands in the moonlight and a few kisses?' he asked cruelly. 'I told you that you were an adolescent with no idea of what it was all about, didn't I, Louise? If you're in such a hurry to grow up, it's time you faced the fact that that boy wants you, as a man wants a woman ... and I don't just mean kisses, Louise.'

'Shut up,' she said furiously. 'Shut up, Daniel!'

'It was written all over his face just now,' he went on ruthlessly. 'He was shaking with it, and you know it. You felt it as much as I did. He could hardly keep his hands off you—even his sister saw that.'

She leapt up, kicking sand into his face, and ran towards the cliffs, wildly seeking any escape from the remorseless cold voice which had been drilling icy facts into her ears.

There were small caves at the end of the first ledge of the cliff. She scaled the cliff with lithe agility and ran into one of them, shivering as the dark clammy air hit her sun-heated body. Tears were running down her face. She stood, her feet shivering on the cold stone cave floor, rubbing her face to halt the tears.

Daniel loomed behind her and she turned, her heart wild as an imprisoned bird. 'Go away!' she shouted at him, and the echo bounced back all around them.

He said nothing, reaching for her. 'No,' she said hoarsely as his face came down.

'I've had enough torture for one day,' he said grimly. 'Let's see if you can take some too, Louise ...'

The hard mouth imprisoned her shaking lips, burning like the sun against them, forcing them relentlessly apart, the consuming heat he produced in her sending shock waves all over her body. She fought him, struggling, twisting, her hands pushing at his chest, her head pulling back evasively.

The powerful hands rested on her bare back, yanking her towards him until their bodies pressed close together. The touch of his skin had an electrifying effect on her, magnetising her, so that her struggles slowly weakened and she gave a faint moan under the fire of his mouth, yielding.

Her hands moved up his bare chest to cling to his shoulders. Her slender limbs were suddenly languorous, heavy with pleasure, lying against him without protest. His kiss deepened, the first violence passing out of it, and a deep urgency, an insistent demand, came into it. Louise was unconscious of everything now, returning his kisses, her hands round his neck, buried deep within the sea-wet hair.

His hands were moving restlessly over the salt-sleek young back, caressing her hungrily. She felt them suddenly seize her waist and push her away from him, holding her by the bare tanned midriff, staring down into her face.

Breathing erratically, she stared up at him, her small face glimmering in the shadowy cave.

'You see how easy it would be for me to take you, Louise,' he said thickly. 'You're no match for any man, let alone me—even a boy like young Blare could take you without difficulty, and it would be too late afterwards to wish you had had more sense. Let this be a lesson to you. Stay within safe bounds, for God's sake. I don't want to see him touching you like that again, do you hear?'

Louise was struggling to regain her self-control, the heat in her body almost overwhelming. She could no more have answered him than she could have flown.

Daniel stared down into her eyes, his face wearing a hard flush. 'God,' he said suddenly, his voice hoarse, 'don't you know yet what effect that lovely body of yours can have on a man? Don't let young Blare near you. You silly little girl, you've already gone to his head. Given the right time and place, he'll go crazy!'

She bent her head, her black hair swishing against her bare shoulders.

'Do you hear me?' he asked furiously.

'Yes, Daniel,' she said, weak with love, utterly submissive to anything he asked of her.

He lifted her chin with a finger, staring into her blue eyes, and she looked at him shyly.

'Did I frighten you?' he asked huskily.

She dropped her eyes. 'A little.'

'But you knew I wouldn't go to the limit,' he said flatly. 'You knew damned well you were safe with me. Think how frightened you'd be if that boy got out of hand when there was nobody else around.'

She didn't answer.

Daniel shook her angrily. 'Or do you imagine

you'd enjoy it? Do you want him, too, Louise?'

'No,' she said quickly, blushing. 'No.'

'Then you'll stay out of danger,' he said, after a pause. 'Make sure his sister's always around. And no more of the sort of thing I had to watch just now. You can't let a man hold you almost naked in his arms and expect to walk away untouched, Louise.'

She nodded, then, on an impulse, leaned her face against his shoulder, kissing his skin. He jerked away, but she whispered shyly, 'You've taught me everything else, Daniel. Teach me this.'

There was a silence so intense she began to tremble, her eyes on the cave floor.

Flushing hotly, she added quickly, 'I mean teach me the sort of things my mother would have taught me ... how can I know how to treat Peter without getting in too deep unless someone tells me? You're angry with me and it isn't fair. I'm not trying to provoke Peter into ... into anything ... how am I to know how he feels?'

Daniel's voice was dry as he replied. 'The first thing you're going to have to learn is how to phrase your invitations, Louise.'

Her face was so hot it burned.

'We'd better go back to the others,' Daniel said. 'God knows what they think we're doing in here.' He pushed her towards the mouth of the cave quite gently. Behind her, he said softly, 'As to your need for lessons in womanhood, we'll take it as it comes, shall we? If you need advice, I'm always here, you know that.'

When they came down the cliff face they found Peter and Sally on the beach, staring at them accusingly.

'We've been exploring some of the caves,' Daniel said casually. 'It was cooler in there, and sometimes there are bats to be found.'

'Bats ... ugh!' Sally shrieked.

Daniel grinned at her, producing a piece of wet seaweed from behind his back. He had found it on a rock as they came down, dropped there by one of the earlier visitors perhaps. Now he trailed it over Sally's arm, making her scream with excited fear.

'They flutter about, squeaking,' he said teasingly, and she fled, her hands over her ears.

Peter looked at Louise jealously. 'How's your cramp?'

'Better,' she said, smiling politely.

'Why don't we get dressed and go into Weston,' Daniel suggested as Sally came back towards them, still laughing.

'Yes, that would be fun,' Sally agreed, always willing to fall in with whatever plans he suggested.

She and Louise changed in the cave and came back to the other two looking fresh and tidy, their damp bikinis in their hands.

They climbed back over the cliff and made their way to the car, then drove along the narrow toll road through the woods which took them back to Weston-super-Mare. Through the trees fringing the winding road they saw the gleam of the blue sea. 'Like your eyes,' Peter whispered to Louise. In the driving mirror she caught the ironic, cold flick of Daniel's eyes and she knew he had overheard. Deliberately she looked back, her glance innocent, and he made a face at her.

They wandered around the holiday resort, thread-ing between the busy crowds, arguing over the

assorted offers of postcards and funny hats, buying
icecream and eating it as they walked. There were
donkeys on the sands. Sally at once set up a clamour
to ride on one, and Daniel with an indulgent glance
at Louise said, 'Why not?'

Louise had always had a donkey ride on their
visits in the past. Today she left her shoes with Peter
and sat, bare-legged, bare-footed, on the rough sandy
back of the donkey, slowly lumbering along the fine
sands.

Daniel came forward to lift her down, his hands
hard on her waist. She felt a terrible temptation as
he released her—a driving desire to lean forward and
kiss him. He stared at her ironically, as if he could
read the thought in her mind, and she turned away to
link her hand in Peter's arm. He knelt to slide her
shoes back on to her feet with a grin.

'Your slippers, Cinderella ... now the girl is mine.'

Over his fair head her eyes met Daniel's cool,
assessing glance, and her heart beat wildly.

They ended the long summer day with dinner in
the town. The candles on the table flickered as the
waiter moved around them. A small band played on
a raised dais, their rhythmic beat soft. Peter had
caught the sun, his fair-skinned face very flushed, his
eyes sleepy after the long day in the open air. Louise
was very quiet, her eyes filled with drowsy happiness.
Daniel added some more wine to her glass, his
fingers brushing hers, and the faint contact made her
weak with delight.

Sally was exuberant. 'What a fantastic day,' she
said as they drove home. 'The best ever, isn't it,
Louise?'

'Yes,' Louise said softly. In the driving mirror her

eyes met Daniel's and she made no attempt to hide the weak languor of the way she looked back at him. His eyes narrowed, then flicked away abruptly. He was silent for the rest of the drive.

CHAPTER FIVE

THE holiday weather continued in the same warm, lazy fashion day after day, and Louise and her two guests enjoyed it without much expense of energy, lounging in the shady park under the oaks, wandering around near the stream, fishing in a desultory way, riding in the early mornings before the sun was too hot.

'This is Paradise,' Sally declared in her exaggerated way. 'And I'm going to hate to leave it. You're so lucky, Louise, to live here all the time.'

Daniel was at work that day. Peter was lying on the banks of the stream, a newspaper over his face, sleeping while he pretended to be fishing. Louise and Sally were lying on the short, warm turf, watching the shadow of the few small clouds pass over the green park as the sun swam in and out of them.

'Why on earth hasn't your brother ever married?' Sally asked her suddenly. 'He's the sexiest man I've ever met, handsome, rich and definitely eligible. That Barbara creature ... the Barracuda he brings here now and then ... she's crazy about him, isn't she? At his age, you would expect him to have been married for years.'

'It isn't the sort of question one can ask,' Louise shrugged with a pretence of indifference.

'I'd ask Peter,' Sally giggled.

'Peter isn't Daniel,' said Louise drily.

'True,' Sally grinned. 'And I'm so glad he isn't ...

tough luck on you, your own brother being so fantastic, but then I suppose he's more a sort of father to you than a brother, being so much older than you.'

With a shock of surprise, Louise realised suddenly that Sally had no idea that Daniel was, in fact, her stepbrother, and no real relation to her at all. During their schooldays it had never come up. Louise had such an intense dislike of discussing her home and Daniel that she had always steered the subject away whenever it came up. When her mother married her stepfather, it had been agreed that Louise should take the family name too, to ease matters, and those who knew the truth of the situation were all local people who might even have forgotten, she thought, after all these years.

Sally sighed. 'No chance for me, of course. I'm not in his class. He's the sophisticated kind and he likes his women to be dazzling, like the Barracuda.'

Louise grinned, enjoying this description of Barbara. 'I know next to nothing about his personal life. Daniel keeps his secrets.'

'I bet they're sensational, though,' Sally groaned. 'He has such sexy eyes.'

Louise lowered her lids, her face expressionless, remembering the times Daniel had kissed her, making her forcibly aware of his expertise and understanding of how to awaken sensation in any female he held in his arms. He had had an easy victory with her, of course. She was fathoms deep in love so long ago. But even had she been unconscious of him before he touched her, she would have felt that flame light in the centre of her body under his compelling hands. He had a strong sexual drive beneath his charming manners, and she found it very odd that all these years he had never married. Sally was right—it was strange. Recalling the night she had seen him making love to a pretty blonde, she wondered if her own jealous, frightened reaction had influenced him. It seemed impossible that the jealousy of a small child could have swayed him, yet certainly she never again saw him at Queen's Dower with any woman. The women he knew were, from that night onward, kept strictly off limits; she had only known of them from chance pieces of gossip, photographs in newspapers, an occasional glimpse of him with them while she was in the village.

It was something of a struggle now to recapture the sweet innocence of her childhood relationship with him—the total confidence, the love, the shared response. It had all seemed so permanent until last year. Daniel had said to her that all adolescents rebelled against their fathers, or became jealously attached to them—for a few seconds she considered the possibility that her feelings for him were merely a temporary phase in her development, a crush she would grow out of. She wildly wished she could believe it. It would be easier to bear than this nagging ache for him.

She seemed to have undergone a radical change in the last few weeks. She had come home so radiantly certain, so sure of him, and he had cruelly shattered her illusions the first evening by spending it with Barbara. Hot colour swept into her face. Jealousy tore at her. She refused to dwell on the visions of that night; they were too bitter.

Ever since she had been riding on a switchback, first up then down, never certain of her own emotions or of his, her head dizzy with a delirium she could not soothe away by cold common sense.

Peter joined them, a little bored, slightly sullen.

'Caught anything?' Sally asked, tongue in cheek, her eyes teasing him.

'Those fish have a sixth sense,' he complained.

'He didn't catch anything,' Sally said ironically to Louise.

'Oh, shut up,' he snapped, pushing her lightly.

They quarrelled like children at times, reverting rapidly to a state of childish warfare which was a hangover from their younger days.

'Oh, it's tragic,' Sally groaned, staring through the dancing sunlight at Queen's Dower, the mellow red façade like a mirage in the heat haze.

'What is?' Louise asked lazily.

'That we have to go home soon,' Sally said.

'You're flying off to Switzerland,' Louise reminded her. 'That can't be bad.'

'You never go abroad, do you?' Sally asked curiously. 'I often used to wonder why. I thought maybe you couldn't afford it, but having seen this I guess you just never wanted to leave it.'

Louise didn't answer, smiling secretly, aware that it was as much Daniel she could not bear to leave as the house, much as she loved the place.

That evening Louise helped Mr and Mrs Duckett to cook dinner, a little tired of talking to Peter and Sally, finding the strain of avoiding Peter's pressing attentions rather wearying. She shelled peas and sliced runner beans, leaning back in a kitchen chair, her slight figure boyish in old jeans and a thin blue shirt.

'Be nice and quiet when they've gone,' Ducky said

with a rather insinuating grin. 'You can stop playing hard to get for a while.'

Louise gave her a dignified look, her small oval face haughty. 'I don't know what you mean.'

'No, of course not,' said Ducky. 'Will, have you finished those potatoes? Get me some mint from the garden, will you?'

Her husband went off, winking at Louise as he walked out. Ducky retrieved the roast lamb and basted it carefully, then replaced it in the oven.

'Hot in here with that oven on,' she said, propping the door a little wider. The fragrance of the herbs came up from the garden below. They had a musky, smoky fragrance, she thought, pungent and sharp.

Sally and Peter were in their rooms quietly reading and listening to the radio. Louise sensed that all three of them were finding the continued presence of the others something of a strain. At first it had been great fun, but now she was eagerly awaiting their departure, longing to be alone again in the great quiet park, the sleepy trees ringing the house like sentries.

Daniel came in a few moments later, with Barbara, saying casually, 'Enough for one extra tonight, Ducky?'

'Of course,' Ducky said without expression, her face wearing that hard look dislike always gave it. She detested Barbara and did not care who knew it.

Louise went on preparing the mint sauce, chopping mint lightly, her slender wrists agile. Barbara gave her a bright, meaningless smile. 'Helping out, Louise?'

'Yes,' said Louise.

Barbara's dark eyes drifted over the boyish figure

in shabby jeans and shirt, and she smiled again. 'Back to the schoolgirl again, are we?' Malice sparkled in her voice.

Louise took no notice, but Ducky slammed a cupboard door · shut, her figure bristling. Daniel glanced at Louise obliquely, his blue-green eyes resting briefly on her slender figure.

He politely removed Barbara from the kitchen. When they were out of earshot, Ducky muttered under her breath. 'Coming here, pricing everything from the jam jars to the portraits ... a mind like a calculator and twice as ugly!'

Louise gave her a sudden, brilliant smile. 'Darling Ducky,' she said gratefully.

Ducky eyed her without comment. 'Humm,' she said at last, shaking her head. 'None so blind as those that won't see.'

Dinner was a very polite, very tense occasion. Barbara held the centre of the table, drawing both Peter and Daniel into talk, flattering them both, teasing them both, her dark eyes smiling.

Sally was sulky, eating her food without much appetite, her bronze head bent over her plate. Louise ate sparingly, saying little, feeling very tired. Daniel glanced at her once or twice, his eyes shrewd, but said nothing.

When Barbara left, there was a hiatus for half an hour, while the three young people talked lazily in arm chairs, sometimes yawning.

'It must be the air here,' said Sally. 'I seem to get tired very early.'

'A good idea,' said Louise. 'Early to bed, early to rise ... we'll ride before breakfast, shall we?'

'Our very last day tomorrow,' Sally sighed. 'I've

had such a good time. I'm very grateful you asked us here, Louise.'

'I'm very glad you came,' she said politely.

Daniel came back from saying goodnight to Barbara with a faint smear of her scarlet lipstick on his mouth. Louise glanced at him, saw it, and felt the knife of pain turn inside her. She looked away without speaking.

He lounged against the door, eyeing them all, a faint ironic smile on his hard lips. 'You look as if you're dead on your feet, all of you,' he commented.

'We've been out in the park all day,' Sally sighed. 'Oh, it's so gorgeous out there in this weather.'

'It will be equally gorgeous in Switzerland,' he teased her.

'Why shouldn't Louise come with us to Switzerland?' Peter asked abruptly, looking at him directly. 'She ought to go abroad. Queen's Dower's very nice, but there's more to life than that.'

Daniel stiffened. He slowly turned cold eyes upon Louise. 'Do you want to go abroad?' he asked her.

She shook her head. For a few jealous seconds she had almost said she did, to ease the pain she felt because she knew he had been kissing Barbara, but then she had thought of leaving Queen's Dower for weeks, and she had known it was too much to bear.

She smiled politely at Peter. 'It's awfully kind of you, Peter, but I couldn't ...'

Peter looked at her, his eyes oddly intense, then he got up and walked out of the room without a word.

Sally gave an amused gasp. 'Oh, dear, his heart is broken!' She grinned at Louise. 'He's been leading up to that ever since we got here, but I told him you'd never agree. He was agog at the thought of getting

you out there alone in the ice and snow.' Her eyes
danced. 'Poor Peter, all his hopes blasted ... he'll
positively die of frustration!' She got up, yawning.
'I think I'll go to bed, too. Goodnight!'

Alone, Louise got up slowly, aware of Daniel
watching her. She walked to the door, but he closed
it and leaned against it. Their eyes met.

'I'm glad you were sensible,' he said quietly. 'I
gather you've been keeping him at arms' length, as I
told you. I think we can consider your baptism of
fire over. One more day and he'll go out of your life
for good.'

She lowered her eyes, bristling with resentment. He
came back in here with Barbara's lipstick on his
mouth and crowed because she had obediently kept
Peter at bay. It was too insufferable!

Quietly, she said, 'I'm still thinking of going to art
school in London.'

Daniel studied her. 'Bristol is where you're going,'
he said coolly. 'And that's settled.'

'Not by me,' she retorted.

'No,' he said. 'By me. And you'll do as I tell you.'

She raised her chin rebelliously. 'Why should I?
I'll be eighteen soon, out of your care.'

'Legally, not financially,' he said drily. 'You do
realise that I'll have to subsidise any grant you may
get pretty substantially? With your background
you're not eligible for public funds. I shall be your
main source of support for the years while you're at
college.'

It had never occurred to her. She stared at him,
flushing. A wild rage in her voice, she said, 'Then I
won't go to college. I'll get a job ... in London.'

Daniel's brows drew together. 'Stop it right there,'

he said tightly. 'I won't have any more of these childish scenes, Louise. I'm not suddenly being turned into some sort of tyrant just because I won't let you have all your own way. I'm doing what I know is best for you.' His eyes flared. 'Don't worry. There are plenty of good-looking boys at Bristol.'

His sarcastic tone stung. 'May I go to bed, please?' she asked him politely, coldly.

He glared at her, then pulled open the door. Louise walked out without looking at him.

The final day of the holiday was as glorious as the preceding ones. Sally was variable, swinging wildly from euphoric pleasure in the place and weather to a regretful gloom that she would soon be leaving it. Peter was oddly quiet, his brown eyes intent whenever Louise looked in his direction, making her feel uneasy. Her deliberate avoidance of his company alone over the last few days had not gone unnoticed. Peter was not stupid. When Sally, groaning, went upstairs to change for dinner, he looked at Louise pleadingly.

'Come for a drive with me before dinner,' he said. 'Please. I've barely seen you alone for days and tomorrow I'll be gone.'

Daniel had not returned from Bristol. She thought of the lipstick on his mouth after he had said goodnight to Barbara, of his cold determination that she should stay away from Peter, and something inside her hardened.

'Why not?' she asked, shrugging.

Daniel had given her a little blue Mini last birthday. She rarely used it, but it had been useful during this holiday, since Peter had enjoyed driving the two girls around in it when they went out.

They drove out of the park and turned down narrow country lanes, the gathering summer dusk filled with moths in the car headlights. The pungent odour of wild garlic filled their nostrils as they suddenly parked beside a shadowy little wood a few miles from Queen's Dower.

Louise turned anxiously towards Peter. 'We ought to get back,' she said, abruptly aware of the folly of her behaviour. 'Dinner will be ready.'

'Louise,' Peter began shakily, his hands reaching towards her.

She pushed him away, trying to smile. 'Come on, Peter ... Daniel will be livid if we're late for dinner.'

'Damn Daniel,' he muttered, his face flushing.

Before she could think of anything else to say or do, he had caught her, leaning over her, his long young body hard against her, forcing her head back against the seat. His mouth found hers hotly, eagerly, and she decided, feeling very cool-headed and alert, that it would be best not to react at all. She lay passively while he kissed her, his breathing very rapid, but he mistook her passivity for encouragement, and his eagerness mounted.

With a shock she felt his hands touching her breasts, and stiffened. 'No,' she said under her breath, beginning to struggle.

'I love you,' Peter said fiercely, holding her body beneath him by force. The trembling fingers caressed her breasts and she felt a wave of terrible alarm and panic. She hit out at him, struggling.

He grabbed at her body again, and suddenly the thin shirt she was wearing tore with a sound that sent positive terror racing in her veins. Wild and shaking, she fought in earnest. Peter was gasping, his hands sliding over the naked skin exposed by her ripped shirt.

'You're so beautiful,' he muttered. 'I'm crazy about you, Louise. Let me ... please, let me ...'

She screamed then, realising just how serious he was, and jerked up a hand to claw at his face. He reeled back, scratched badly, and hit his head on the windscreen. While he was off balance she slid out of the car and ran into the wood.

She ran without looking back or hesitating, turning into the deepest part of the wood. She knew it vaguely, knew which direction it ran in, but in the gathering dusk it was hard to see where one was going, and she tripped over an exposed root and lay, her face grazed and smeared with leaf mould, listening to the crashing sound of Peter tearing after her. Gathering her wits together, she glanced around her and saw a spreading expanse of bracken, already beginning to turn brown at the edges as summer advanced. She crawled into it and lay, hidden, her heart leaping, hearing Peter coming towards her.

'Louise!' His voice had a panic-stricken note. 'Darling, I'm sorry ... I won't hurt you ... come back!'

She thought for a moment of going out to him, then she remembered the way he had touched her after he tore her shirt, and she lay very still, like a frightened little animal, not daring to make a sound or give him any clue as to her whereabouts.

He crashed on past the bracken, hearing the distant snap of a twig which he took to be her footstep. Louise lay, shaking, suddenly very chilled.

Peter's sudden violence had petrified her. The way

he breathed, the way he touched her, had sent waves of cold shock to her head. She was incapable of moving at the moment, her slender body shuddering.

Peter came back, still calling her. He was beginning to be angry now. She heard an almost savage note in his voice as he shouted a curse at her. 'Stay there, then, you little bitch!' he bellowed. 'You teased me until I grabbed for you, then you turned me down ... stay there all night for all I care!'

He stalked back to the car and she heard the engine start in the distance. Then it died again. He got out, slamming the door, and she began to shake again, terrified.

'Louise!' he called hoarsely. 'Louise, I'm sorry ... come out, please. I won't hurt you. You know I won't hurt you. You can't stay here—it's getting dark and it's cold.'

He waited for an answer but she made none. His savage outburst earlier had convinced her she could not trust him. They were alone in this silent, dark wood, and Louise was terrified of him.

She heard him swearing under his breath. Slowly he went back to the car. The engine started again and at last the car drove away. She relaxed, every limb in her body shivering with fright and cold. The summer night seemed to surround her.

At last she sat up and pulled together the torn shirt. Her skin felt clammy to the touch. Her hair was full of leaves, her face was filthy. She got up and slowly began to move towards the road, then halted. Peter might come back; he might be waiting just out of earshot. She bit her lower lip, wondering what on earth to do.

What would Peter do? Would he wait? Or would

he go back to the house and confess everything to
Daniel?

She winced at that thought. Daniel would kill him.

Suddenly she heard a blundering among the trees
and that birdlike panic flared inside her again. Peter,
she thought, beginning to run. Blind in the dark, she
fled straight into a tree and crashed her head against
it, falling stunned and bleeding to the mossy ground.

She lost consciousness, and when she came to again
she could not for a moment remember where she was,
a tremulous sense of alienation and fear inside her.
Her eyes fluttered blindly upwards. The trees pressed
in all round her, breathing softly in the summer wind.
Little cracks and rustlings seemed very loud.

Slowly her memory returned and she sat up, winc-
ing as her head stabbed with pain.

How long had she lain here? A few moments? Or
longer? She was not wearing a watch. She had no
idea. Holding on to the tree trunk, she staggered to
her feet. Her head swam. She closed her eyes, giddy
and sick.

It was then that she heard the car engine, heard it
slow and stop. Her heart thundered with the return
of that terrible panic. She looked around her desperately, trying to find somewhere to hide.

Then she recognised the voice. 'Louise!' It was a
stark imperative, a command, a furious demand that
she come out.

'I'm here!' she called, her voice trembling.

He came towards her very fast, parting trailing
brambles which had earlier scratched her face, finding his way through the narrow hidden paths with
the instinct of one born among these woods.

Before he got to her his voice lashed at her, filled

with rage and menace. 'My God, I could kill you, you stupid blind child! I warned you. Just let me get my hands on you!'

He halted as he reached her, shining a flashlight on her. It wavered in his hand, the blinding light quivering, as by it he took in her condition.

'God!' He sounded so violent she began to shake again, weeping bitterly, her head bowing into her hands.

Daniel swung her up into his arms and walked back to the car, carrying her cradled against his shoulder. Her tears flooded out on to his chest, her slender body shook wildly with the force of her weeping.

He pulled a tartan rug out from the back of the car and wrapped her into it roughly, then he started the car and drove back to Queen's Dower, a fixed grim look on his face.

Louise cried all the way home, sobs rending her. The pain in her head was like a hot spike driven into her brain. Her knees stung and her palms were aching.

When they reached the house he carried her, still wrapped in the tartan rug, into the private apartments. Ducky was waiting, a tense expression on her round doll's face. She clucked as she saw them, relief in her eyes.

'Is she all right?'

'No,' Daniel said bitingly, 'she bloody well isn't ... have they gone?'

'Will drove them to Bristol to catch a train,' Ducky said.

'That saves me having to face a charge of murder,' Daniel said between his teeth. 'A pity, though. I'd have got a kick out of beating that boy's brains out!'

They took Louise into the bedroom and Ducky exclaimed in shock as she saw the deep graze on her forehead, the dark blood drying on it already.

'Ring the doctor,' Daniel snapped.

'I'll look after her while you ring him,' said Ducky.

He turned a menacing look on her. 'Do as you're damn well told,' he said fiercely.

Ducky silently went out.

Louise was still crying, but quietly now, shuddering with sobs which wrenched her body. Daniel unwrapped the blanket. She grabbed for it, shivering.

'Let it go, Louise,' he said forcefully.

Without looking at him she dropped her fingers away. He unravelled it and stared down at her slight body. Her blue shirt was ripped and covered with earth. Her jeans were torn at the hem and knee, stained where she had fallen. Her face was almost unrecognisable beneath the leaf mould, tear stains and scratch marks on it.

Silently Daniel turned away and opened a drawer, finding a nightdress. Returning to her, he bent and began to remove her shirt. She gave a wild, hoarse cry of refusal, her eyes panic-stricken.

'It's Daniel, Louise,' he said calmly. 'Let me put your nightdress on, darling.'

The quiet tone reached her. She sat quiescent while he pulled off the shirt and dropped the nightdress over her head, his blue-green eyes flicking swiftly over the visible dark bruises on her white skin.

'Take off your jeans,' he told her.

Ducky came back into the room. 'Doctor's on his way,' she said, looking sharply at Louise's white, stained face.

'Get her jeans off,' Daniel said crisply.

He went out and returned in a moment with a bowl of warm water and a sponge. Gently he sponged away the stains of tears, dirt and blood from her face. She lifted her face like an obedient child as he slowly dabbed it dry, taking care not to hurt her.

'Her knees are bleeding,' Ducky said tightly.

Daniel knelt and bathed them too, inspecting the bramble scratches and grazed calves.

Under her breath, Ducky said, 'How did she get in a state like this? My God, what did that boy do to her?'

Daniel's face was terrifying. He said nothing, but his grim, white features glared down at Louise. She had stopped crying now, her eyes closed in mute misery, her head back against the chair she sat in, her scratched hands on her knee.

The doctor arrived and took a look at her, shaking his head over her injuries. 'What happened?'

'We don't know yet,' Daniel said grimly. 'When we do, I'll deal with it personally.'

'She must have an X-ray,' the doctor said. 'That head took a nasty bang. She may have concussion.'

'She's in shock,' Daniel said tightly. 'I'll take her there myself.'

'She should stay there overnight,' the doctor said.

'No.' Daniel brooked no argument. 'She's coming home once she's had it.'

'You're taking a serious risk,' the doctor said irritably.

'If the X-ray shows signs of damage, she can stay, otherwise she's coming home at once,' Daniel told him.

Louise barely noticed the trip to the hospital.

Dazed, silent, hollow-eyed, she sat with Daniel at her side throughout the time. When they were back at the house Daniel slid her into bed, made her drink hot milk and take some pills. As he snapped off the light she came alive for a second.

'Daniel . . .' Her voice was filled with shaking panic.

Quietly out of the dark he said, 'I'm not going anywhere. I'll be here.'

She tried to peer at him through the darkness of the room. He was sitting in a chair near her bed, a shadowy shape she did not recognise, but the calm sound of his voice eased her. She lay down and sighed. Slowly she fell asleep.

CHAPTER SIX

WHEN she awoke the room was shadowy although she could hear the sound of birds out in the park. The curtains were still drawn, but the sun spilled through in golden streaks, indicating that it was late in the day. Her lids fluttered around the room and met Daniel's watchful eyes. He was still sitting in the same chair, and there was a dark shadow of stubble on his chin, showing her that he had not even shaved this morning.

He got up quietly and came to the bed, laying a hand on her temple. Without a word he lifted her wrist after that, his face cool as he took her pulse. Only after he had laid her hand down did he ask her quietly, 'How do you feel?'

'My head aches a bit,' she whispered.

He nodded. 'Hungry?'

She shook her head, her lower lip quivering.

Daniel sat down on the edge of the bed, taking her hands in his own and slowly rubbing them, as if she were chilled and he was putting warmth into her.

'Would you like a cup of tea?'

She nodded.

He released her hands and went out. A moment later he came back and sat down again, staring down at her, his eyes distant.

'Can you tell me about it now?'

The hot, betraying colour filled her face and she looked away.

'Take your time,' he said gently. 'It's all over now. You're quite safe. Just tell me in your own way.'

'We went for a drive,' she whispered. 'Just for a few minutes, he said. He stopped by the wood and tried to kiss me and I said no.' Her voice trembled and she swallowed. 'But he wouldn't stop. I tried to stop him, but he pulled at me, and my shirt tore ...'

Ducky came into the room with a cup of tea then, and Daniel took it with a nod. Ducky looked down at her with a loving, concerned smile.

'How are you, cherub? Poor little face, it's so scratched!'

Daniel gave her a curt nod. 'Later, Ducky,' he said tautly.

She looked at him sharply, then shrugged and went out.

'Go on,' Daniel said harshly. 'What happened after he tore your shirt?'

Louise was crimson, shuddering, her eyes on the wall, her lip shaking. 'I ... he ... I was frightened ... I ran...'

'You've left out the bit that interests me,' Daniel said bitingly. He put a hand to her chin and forced her to look at him, his opalescent eyes filled with flame.

'Start again, Louise, and I want it all this time. What did he do?'

'Nothing,' she whispered shakily.

His hand tightened. 'Louise! Don't give me that!'

'Don't, Daniel,' she whimpered. 'You're hurting me.'

'I'd like to kill you,' he muttered fiercely through his teeth.

Oddly, this made her half laugh, slightly hysterical.

'I can't,' she whispered, twisting her head away.

He put both hands around her face, framing it, tilting it to face him.

'Now,' he said tautly. 'Let's have it, all of it. What did he do?'

'It wasn't what he did,' she cried, angry now. 'It was ...' She took a deep breath. 'It was what I saw he was going to do if I didn't get away.'

Daniel sat back, still holding her face, staring deep into her eyes. 'He touched you.'

She didn't answer, her face hot, her eyes shamed.

'I saw the bruises,' he said tightly.

Stumblingly, she said, 'He ... he was excited.'

Daniel swore under his breath.

'He asked me to ... to let him, so I hit him. He banged his head on the windscreen and I was able to get away. I ran into the wood and fell over, so I hid in the bracken until he had gone. Then I was going to come home, but I heard a noise that frightened me. I thought he might have come back, so I ran, and I must have run into a tree ... the next thing I knew was you were calling me.'

'Have you left anything out?' he asked between his teeth.

Louise shook her head, her eyes held by his.

There was a long silence, then he slowly handed her the cup of tea. 'Drink that.'

She sipped it, cupping her trembling hands around it, staring at the liquid as she drank.

After a long silence, Daniel commented, 'Well, we're both lucky.'

'Both?' she asked, her eyes surprised.

His face was like flint. 'If he'd had you I'd have

killed him with my bare hands. As it is, I'm saved the trouble.'

She flushed, looking away. 'When he came back and told you ... what did you do?'

'I smashed his teeth down his throat,' Daniel said grimly. 'He only told me a small part of the truth, but that was enough.'

She flinched. 'What did he say?'

'That he'd parked and tried to kiss you, and you'd panicked and run into the woods,' Daniel said grittily. 'I knew damned well there had to be more than that, but I couldn't waste time then arguing about it, so I found out exactly where he last saw you, then I knocked him from one side of the room to the other, told Will to take him and his damned sister to Bristol Station and drove like a fiend to find you.'

'Poor Sally,' she said weakly. Then, with a shiver, 'Poor Peter!'

Daniel was silent and she looked at him unhappily. 'It was my fault,' she whispered. 'I let him kiss me before.'

'I warned you,' Daniel said flatly. 'He had a bad case, and you were blind not to see it.'

'I'm sorry,' she faltered, beginning to cry again.

He removed her cup and gathered her into his arms, his face against her hair. 'That's enough,' he said huskily. 'You've learnt your lesson. You got away by the skin of your teeth, and you got hurt, but you won't make that mistake again. We have to pay for our experiences.'

'I'll never let a man touch me again,' she whimpered, leaning against him.

Daniel gave a soft sound of dry amusement, his

lips brushing her cheek. 'There's no need for such extreme action. Just give yourself a breathing space before you make any drastic decisions like that.'

'I mean it,' she said fiercely. The wild blue eyes were glittering in her pale, tearstained face. 'I hated it, the way he looked at me, the way he touched me.' She shuddered. 'I can hear him breathing now ... horrible!'

Daniel surveyed her oddly, his eyes narrowed. 'His technique was obviously faulty,' he said drily.

She looked at him incredulously. 'It isn't funny!'

Daniel was watching her, his face unreadable. 'When I made love to you I got a response like a tidal wave,' he said coolly.

Her face ran with wild colour. 'Oh!' she said, breathless, angry, shamed. She looked round the room, as though looking for somewhere to hide, then dived under the bedclothes and pulled them over her head.

She heard Daniel laugh softly, then he patted the heaving bump that was her head.

'You'd better stay in bed until the doctor says you can get up,' he said calmly. 'Sleep well, Louise.'

She heard the door close behind him before she sat up, her face filled with seething emotion. He had been laughing at her ... when he stopped being angry with Peter, he had suddenly become amused. Why? How could he be so cruel, so beastly?

She did not see Daniel again until next morning. The doctor had visited her, smiled over her, pronounced her perfectly fit but told her to stay in bed for another day to get over the shock of her accident. Daniel walked into her room after breakfast next day, looking calmly efficient in his office suit.

He dropped two opened letters on the bed. Louise glanced at them, to hide her embarrassed reaction at seeing him, and saw that although addressed to her they had been read.

She glanced at him questioningly.

'I wasn't going to let you read anything that might upset you,' he explained coolly.

She took out the brief notes. One was from Peter, the other from Sally. They were both apologetic. Over the one from Sally she bit her lip, reading the shock her friend had received. Peter had written a stiff little epistle in which she saw his true feelings— he felt she had led him on and then rejected him, and it stung.

She looked nervously at Daniel. 'Peter called me a tease,' she said jerkily. 'When he got mad, I mean.'

'As a chauvinist of the first water, I can see his point,' Daniel observed drily.

She gave him a little scowl. 'Letting someone kiss you doesn't mean they can do as they like!'

'No,' he said in hard amusement, 'so it seems.'

'Oh, you're insufferable!' she cried.

'I told you you had a lot to learn,' he said, smiling.

'You're beginning to sound as if you sympathise with Peter,' she said flatly.

'You did lead him up the garden path,' he observed.

'Why did you hit him, then?' she asked.

The blue-green eyes glittered. 'For scaring you out of your silly little wits,' he said brusquely. 'If you'd let him kiss you, that would have been different. But he panicked you and then left you alone at night in a damned wood. So I let fly at him. I felt terrified myself as I drove there. Anything could have happened to you, left alone like that, witless and defenceless . . . God knows what might have happened.'

'It's horrible,' she said childishly.

'His father rang to apologise yesterday. He got the story out of Peter, and I think he was torn between irritation with you and disgust with the boy. I was a bit stiff with him, but we parted without words of anger.'

'That's comforting,' she said sarcastically.

'At least now you know why I won't let you go to London,' Daniel said in satisfaction. 'You'll drive into Bristol every day with me and take an art course there.'

She didn't answer, and he looked down at her, his eyes amused. 'Say yes, Daniel,' he prompted teasingly.

She put her tongue out, her face sulky.

He laughed. 'Back to age ten, are we? Well, that's an improvement for a little while.'

'Oh, go to work!' she snapped, her lower lip stubborn.

Daniel went, his manner still amused, and Louise spent the day reading and listening to the radio. In the evening Ducky came into the bedroom and said that Daniel had left word she could get up for dinner if she had been good.

She raged childishly against him as Ducky helped her dress in her white dress. Ducky listened, her eyes sparkling. She brushed the long black hair until it shone and clipped two metallic butterfly slides into it. Louise deliberately added some make-up, despite Ducky's tut of disapproval.

'I've got to disguise these scratches,' Louise said rebelliously, although she knew she was doing it to annoy Daniel.

He was drinking a glass of sherry as she came into the room. He turned, a look of amusement in his eyes, and studied her, the blue-green eyes narrowing.

'Very apt hair decorations,' he commented at last.

Her hand flew up to the butterflies and a blush came into her face, a blush of rage.

'Is Barbara coming to dinner, by any chance?' she asked, her voice deliberately provoking.

'Shall I ring her and ask her to come?' he countered, his smile taunting.

She relapsed into a sulky silence at that. After a pause she asked, 'May I have a glass of sherry, please?'

He gave her one of his cool looks, but poured a little sherry into a very large glass, handing it to her.

'Oh, how generous,' she said, drinking it very fast.

'Dinner's ready,' Ducky said from the door.

Daniel lifted Louise from her chair, his wrist firm. 'Come on, you baby,' he said insufferably.

Louise ate her meal in silence, avoiding his occasional amused looks. Afterwards she sat on the couch listening to a record, flipping over a magazine, her face averted from him.

Ducky and Will went home after doing the washing up, and as she heard their called goodnights Louise felt a sudden rise of panic in her chest. Her colour abruptly deepened to a wild rosé and her eyes became a very bright blue.

Daniel was studying her quizzically as she put down the magazine. 'I think I'll go to bed,' she said nervously.

As she moved towards the door he rose too, and she halted, her face clearly revealing her panic.

His smile disappeared. 'Stop it, Louise,' he ordered in a cold, imperative voice.

'Stop what?' she countered anxiously.

'You know very well what I mean,' he said crisply. 'You're perfectly safe with me and don't pretend to believe otherwise. If you behave like this, I'll get Ducky to stay in the house overnight.'

Her lashes fell. After a pause she whispered, 'I'm sorry.'

'Do you know what you need?' he asked, moving up to her. He took her chin in his hand and smiled into her eyes, charm making him suddenly irresistible. 'What did I make you do when you took your first tumble on that little Shetland pony I bought you when you were six?'

'Get straight back on again,' she said, eyes wide.

He grinned lazily. 'Exactly.'

Her heart began to shake inside her breast and she was suddenly breathless, staring up at him.

He bent forward and lightly, softly, brushed her mouth with his lips. She closed her eyes, pleasure invading her.

'You see?' he said. 'No panic. No problem.'

Reluctantly she opened her eyes and gave him a faint smile. He gently ran a finger down her nose, then trailed it over her mouth.

'Go to bed and sleep like a baby,' he said.

Suddenly her heart was burning, wild with love. She looked at him drowningly, her whole face suffused with colour.

'I love you,' she said, with more intensity than she knew.

Then she turned and walked out of the room and went to bed. Sleep fell on her like a great dark tower, and her dreams were confused and terrifying. She ran through dark, whispering woods, hearing footsteps always behind her, calling for Daniel, who never came.

Then he was there, holding her, shaking her, his face pale and anxious, and she was brought wide awake, trembling, tears in her eyes. He had his arms around her, his hand supporting her head, pushing into the tangled black hair, his fingertips caressing her scalp.

'You were having a nightmare,' he said. 'Are you all right?'

Shuddering, Louise leaned her hot face against him, pushing it into the open collar of his pyjamas, the scent of his skin in her nostrils. 'The wood,' she mumbled. 'So dark, and all the noises ... you didn't come...'

'I'm here,' he soothed, holding her closer, feeling her shake in his arms. 'I'm here now. I'm always here.'

Still locked in the childish grievance of her nightmare she sobbed, 'I needed you. I wanted you, and you didn't come.'

'Darling,' he whispered, pushing her head against himself, stroking her hair. 'I'm here ... I'll always be here ...'

'Don't leave me,' she said, exhausted and suddenly yawning.

'No,' he promised, feeling the limp heaviness of her slender limbs in his arms.

She put her arms around his neck, locking him against her, and let her whole weight fall on him, sleep almost snatching her back into the dark of oblivion, but refusing to release him.

Daniel's fingers were stroking her hair slowly, peacefully, calming her. She felt him lower her to her pillow, but when he tried to unprise her clinging arms they tightened and she moaned, her eyes shut, almost asleep yet aware that he was going. He stopped trying to release himself and she felt his head beside hers on the pillow. Childishly she turned towards him, burrowing against him like a lost small animal. His arms were round her, holding her tightly. Louise felt secure and safe. She let the dark waters of sleep float back over her mind.

When she woke up it was daylight and Ducky was standing there, a dumb incredulous look in her face. Louise gazed at her innocently, baffled, then she suddenly came snapping back to awareness, and realised that she was lying in Daniel's arms, his head above hers on the pillow, his chin on her hair. He was still asleep, but as she moved slightly, her face burning under Ducky's silent stare, Daniel woke abruptly. He looked into Ducky's face and there was a stiff silence.

Without a word Ducky slapped the cup of tea she carried down upon Louise's bedside table, then she turned and walked out, banging the door.

Louise drew away from Daniel's arms and sat up, hardly knowing where to look. She barely remembered her dream last night. She did not remember Daniel trying to free himself very clearly, but she had an impression that she had been crying, that he had held her and comforted her until she went to sleep. Now she was blushing, speechless.

Daniel lay there, very silent, not moving. She had no idea what he was thinking.

At last he said in a clipped voice, 'That's another

fine mess you've gotten me into!'

She giggled, appalled and relieved.

'I'll explain to Ducky about the nightmare,' she said shyly. 'I often used to have them when I was little.'

'As you've been telling me for some time, you're not a little girl any more,' Daniel said coolly. 'You're an extremely sexy and beautiful big girl, and you've just spent the night with me.'

She was covered in confusion, her cheeks burning, partly because he had said she was sexy ... the description threw her, excited her, delighted her.

'Only Ducky knows,' she said. 'She wouldn't tell. Wild horses wouldn't drag it out of her.'

Daniel laughed grimly. 'I'm not spending the next few years face to face with a coldly reproving stare from Ducky,' he said.

'When I tell her about my nightmare ...' she began weakly.

'My sweet innocent, you may be naïve enough to swallow that thin story, but Ducky certainly isn't. Only a short time ago you were carried home after a rape attack.'

'Not rape,' she muttered, sickened.

'All right, an attack of some unspecified kind,' he altered drily. 'Now Ducky finds you in bed with me. She'll be waiting with breathless horror for the next thrilling instalment of your life. From being a sweet little schoolgirl you're turning into Mata Hari!'

'Oh, why are you so horrid to me?' she asked, turning baleful blue eyes on him.

His opalescent eyes danced with amusement. 'My God, you ruin my reputation with my own servants, and ask me why I'm so horrid to you?'

'I didn't ask you to stay all night,' she said, her face very pink.

'Correction,' he drawled. 'You didn't ask—you begged. Don't leave me, Daniel, you pleaded, clinging like a little limpet ...'

'You beast!' she snapped furiously, jerking a hand round to slap him.

He caught it in his fingers, swinging it lightly, staring at her with a curiously lighthearted grin. 'Well, that's your career as an art student gone for a burton,' he observed.

Louise was baffled. 'Why should it?'

'My wife isn't going around covered in paint stains and smelling of linseed oil,' he said smoothly, watching her face.

She was very still, looking at him with very wide, very brilliant blue eyes.

'That isn't funny,' she said at last, her colour all going, and her small oval face peculiarly white.

'It wasn't meant to be,' he drawled. 'Just imagine how Ducky is going to treat me if I don't make an honest woman out of you ... my eggs will be parboiled for the rest of my life, and she'll put salt in my tea ... if I'm lucky. If she really gets nasty it could be white arsenic.'

'Stop it, Daniel,' she muttered, pulling at her wrist to free herself.

'Louise ...' his voice was suddenly sober, 'will you marry me?'

She felt her heart melt, a strange floating sensation in her body. She looked at him in disbelief, longing to believe he meant it.

'You don't want to marry a girl of my age,' she said weakly.

'It's suicidal madness,' he agreed. 'But I'm willing to take the risk if you are.'

She hesitated for another second, then said huskily, 'Yes, Daniel, I'll marry you.' It was what she wanted most in the world. She loved him desperately, and although she was afraid he did not love her like that she knew he did love her, in his way. She would make him happy. Then she thought of Barbara and her small face hardened. Daniel would never be happy with a woman who saw Queen's Dower only in terms of its market value. All her life Daniel had belonged to her. He had promised her as a child that he would always be hers, and Louise was going to hold him to that promise.

She bent down, very grave and extraordinarily young in her brief white nightdress. Her lips brushed softly over his mouth, then, with an abrupt change of mood, she flew away before his hands could come up to hold her, jumping out of bed. 'I must go and tell Ducky before she parboils your eggs,' she said, flying out of the room.

Ducky was moving around the kitchen with a face like thunder. Will was scratching his head, watching his wife, aware with his deep knowledge of her that something was very wrong, but not understanding what.

Louise halted in the doorway, a slender childish figure in the little white nightdress.

Will looked at her in surprise, while his wife turned and stared at her, the round Dutch doll's face stiff.

'Daniel and I are getting married,' Louise said, the words bursting out of her.

Ducky's face melted and the warm eyes grew soft with love. Louise looked at her, her own blue eyes wild with joy, then she turned and ran out again, leaving husband and wife staring at each other.

Her bedroom was empty when she returned to it. She collected her jeans and a clean pink shirt and went into the bathroom. Ten minutes later, dressed and freshly showered, she went to have breakfast and found Daniel there, reading his paper, his expression calm.

She sat down at the table and he looked at her over his paper, his smile quizzical.

'You look very pleased with yourself,' he said softly.

'Can I come into Bristol today?' she asked.

'Why?'

'To order a wedding dress,' she said.

Daniel laughed, his eyes glinting. 'My God, I feel like a roped steer!'

The words were teasing, but the tone was filled with soft amusement.

'There's no family to bother about,' she pointed out, buttering toast efficiently. 'We can have a very quiet wedding.'

'Can I come?' Daniel enquired, drinking his tea.

She hit him with her spoon. 'Just our friends, in the village church, and a party afterwards. I do love parties.' Her smile was beatific. 'We don't even need a honeymoon. There's nowhere nicer than Queen's Dower.'

'I'm glad to see you're going to be a very inexpensive wife,' he commented.

'Do you want to wear morning clothes, or just a lounge suit?' she asked.

'Oh, a morning suit,' he said solemnly. 'I'm only planing to get married once in my life, so I might as well do it in style.'

'Top hat and everything?'

'Absolutely everything,' he agreed. 'Even a bride ... of sorts!'

Louise put out her tongue at him. 'I shall make a very pretty bride, you'll see!'

Daniel's eyes glinted, blue-green and filled with laughter. 'That's one certainty,' he said. 'You'll be the most enchanting bride ever seen, even if the guests do think I snatched you from your nursery school.'

She sobered. Eyeing him anxiously, she asked, 'Daniel, will you mind that very much?'

He considered her through his lashes. 'You'll have to make it worth my while,' he said teasingly, then got up and put his newspaper under his arm. 'I'm going to Bristol in ten minutes. You'd better be ready or I'll go without you.'

CHAPTER SEVEN

Too wrapped up in her own shining happiness, too concerned with Daniel, and too inexperienced to consider any possible repercussions of their decision to marry, Louise was astonished over the next few days to realise what a seemingly endless series of ripples had been set up by the announcement of their engagement.

Daniel had arranged for it to appear in *The Times*. Louise, not having been told beforehand, was flushed with delight when he handed her the paper two days later, tapping the court page on which forthcoming marriages were announced. Wide-eyed, quite unprepared, she glanced where his finger pointed, and a deep rose pink flush grew in her face. 'Oh,' she murmured. 'Why didn't you tell me?'

'A surprise,' he said, his mouth twitching with amusement. 'You did realise we were going to have to let the rest of the world in on our secret, I suppose? I mean, this wasn't to be a dark family secret?'

'Silly,' she smiled, reading the announcement again, her eyes dwelling eagerly on his name.

The telephone began to ring ten minutes later. It rang throughout the day, and Ducky's voice took on a hoarse, irritated ring as she went on answering it. Daniel and Louise were both 'out' all day. Ducky took messages, scrawling them impatiently in her unreadable shorthand which boiled down to a curt abbreviation of everything but the shortest words.

Daniel and Louise went into hysterics over some of them. 'What does Mrs Bl. con. and wh. fl. mean, Ducky?' Daniel asked gravely, while Louise stuffed a handkerchief in her mouth.

Ducky eyed him, her mouth tight. 'The Vicar's wife said give you her congratulations, and will you tell her well in advance whether you'll want her to do the flowers in church or are you having professional florists.'

Daniel grinned, 'Tell her to ask my fiancée.'

'Mrs Blundell will die a million deaths if we get in professional florists,' Louise said wisely. 'She adores doing the flowers for weddings and the extra money you have to pay her makes a useful boost to her housekeeping money.'

'Tell Mrs Blundell we'd love to have her do the flowers,' Daniel informed Ducky.

'Tell her yourself,' Ducky snapped. 'My throat's hoarse—I've been sucking cough sweets all day!'

Reporters began to hover around the closed park gates some time during that day, and Daniel ordered Will to lock them after a photographer was discovered perched, like a rather uncertain, bedraggled owl, in a tree close to the house, attempting to snatch a lens shot of Louise. Marching the man off the premises, one hand at his collar, the other at his back, Daniel threw him through the gates. 'The next trespasser I find on my land will get a stiff peppering of buckshot,' he informed the gathered gentlemen of the press, ignoring the flashbulbs exploding around him. 'Buckshot isn't fatal,' he added, his mouth sardonic, 'but very painful and necessitating long, humiliating hours spent on one's stomach if aimed correctly.'

'Can we have a picture of you and your sister, sir?'

a dwarf-like photographer asked, craning through the gates.

Daniel's eyes blazed and his mouth hardened. 'My *step*sister is no blood relation of mine,' he said furiously. 'No blood relation whatever.'

The questions began showering around him as he turned and stalked back to the house. There was a strained anger in his face as he came into the room, and Louise felt a pang of alarm. 'What's wrong?'

'Nothing,' he said tersely.

'Daniel,' she begged, putting a hand on his shoulder pleadingly, 'tell me.'

His expression was uncertain for a moment, then he brusquely described the incident to her, and she listened soberly, realising at once what had upset him.

'Does it matter what anyone thinks?' she asked him.

'Yes,' he said tautly, 'you know damned well it does. Oh, God, I must have been insane to think I could get away with it!'

Before she could say anything he broke away from her and went out. Louise sat down, sighing, her face anxious.

Ducky came in, groaning. 'The Vicar's on the phone. Must speak to Daniel, but he's just gone off to Bristol. Will you talk to him?'

Louise obediently went off to talk to the Vicar, who was concerned and embarrassed. 'You are very young for such a step, my dear, and, after all Daniel has been a brother to you all your life. I really think we should all have a little chat before you go any further with this plan of marriage.'

She felt a wild burning anger in her veins. The

whole world was against them, she thought, and her voice took on a deep, adult note of cold insistence. 'Vicar, it's very kind of you to be so concerned, but Daniel and I are going to be very happy together. There's absolutely no need for anyone to worry about either of us.'

When she put the phone down Ducky studied her, a glint in her eye. 'Growing up very fast, aren't we?' she commented, satisfaction in her voice. 'You tell them, cherub.'

Louise flew into her arms, hugging her. 'I'll make him happy,' she whispered shakily. 'I will.'

'You always have,' Ducky said oddly, patting her.

The press got tired of waiting when a sudden thunderstorm broke that evening, drenching them all before they got back to their cars. By eight the quiet country lane was deserted again, and the park was filled with a sweet, fresh after-rain smell which percolated to the whole house.

Daniel was late back from Bristol, and while she was waiting for him Louise was suddenly confronted by Barbara, her exquisitely made-up face tight with rage, her voice shrill.

Louise stood up from the chair in which she had been lounging, her jean-clad legs curled under her. Nervously she pulled down her thin shabby yellow sweater, and Barbara's narrowed, sparking eyes followed the movement with a twist of her red lips.

'My God, he must be completely crazy!' Barbara snapped in a high, stiff tone.

Louise said nothing, lifting her rounded chin to meet whatever the older woman meant to say.

'You know why he's marrying you, don't you?' Barbara asked her unpleasantly. 'Because you're so damned young! He's thirty-five, getting near the desperate age, and you've flattered him with that very obvious crush you've got on him ... don't think it wasn't as plain as a pikestaff to everyone who saw the way you looked at him. Any man of his age would be flattered. You're a pretty kid, even if you are only a teenager, and he can't resist taking what you're so desperate to give him.'

Louise felt her face burn with humiliation, but she somehow managed to keep a calm look on her features.

Barbara hadn't finished. Louise's quiet refusal to be flurried into a reply drove her mad.

'You don't think marriage to a child will satisfy a man like Daniel for long, do you? He'll come back to me.' Her dark eyes glared. 'We're lovers, didn't you realise that? He's my lover. And he will be again once he's had all he wants from you!'

The sickness inside Louise was eating at her like acid, but by an effort of extreme will power she kept herself from crying out.

Barbara hissed in her thwarted bitterness, her voice quavering with temper. 'He's only marrying you instead of taking you to bed because you're his bloody stepsister. He can't bring himself to seduce you, so he's marrying you first!'

Louise drew a deep breath to steady herself. 'What makes you think we haven't slept together?' she asked quietly.

The question totally threw Barbara. She stared, her dark eyes almost black. A long silence followed.

'I don't believe you,' she whispered at last, and Louise could see that she was utterly shattered.

She gave Barbara a cool little smile. 'I would tell

you to ask Mrs Duckett, but I'm afraid Ducky would never tell you one of the family secrets.'

Barbara slowly flushed a deep red. 'My God,' she said hoarsely. Louise could see that she believed her, convinced by the quiet careful tone. 'It's disgusting!' Oddly, Barbara looked really shocked. 'It's incest,' she said wildly.

Louise laughed. 'Don't be silly. There's no tie of blood between us—surely you know that?'

Barbara stared at her. 'How long has it been going on? These last few weeks you've had that boy here ... it must have started months ago. Oh, he must be the most devious, the most ...' She broke off, biting her lip. 'I've always known there was something odd about the way he talked about you, the way he spent every minute of his time with you. I thought it was touching, a man of his age being so fond of a kid sister, but all the time ... this!' She shuddered. 'And now he's marrying you.' Her eyes were filled with rage. 'If he's already ...' She broke off, her face white.

Louise knew exactly what was in her mind. There was no need for her to say another word. Calm, her oval face delicately tranquil, she looked back at Barbara and saw jealous spite in her face.

At that moment Daniel walked into the room. His hard features tightened as he saw Barbara, then his opalescent eyes flashed to Louise's face, anxiety in them.

Barbara saw the concerned, intent look he gave the girl, and her fury burst out with renewed vigour.

'Oh, there's no need to look so worried about her,' she shouted. 'She's as calm as a nun. She stood there without a flicker of shame and admitted she's been your mistress for months!'

Daniel's face, filled for a second with incredulous shock, stared at Louise. She met his eyes calmly, no flicker of expression in her features.

Daniel slowly brought his face under control, turning back towards Barbara. 'There's no point in this discussion,' he said. 'I suggest we do the sensible thing and end it now.'

'Not until you tell her you've slept with me too,' Barbara said bitterly. 'Go on, tell the little bitch!'

'I already knew,' Louise said softly.

Daniel's face, white and strained, flicked a look at her and then turned back towards Barbara.

A red spot burned in each of the enamelled cheeks. Barbara drew a long harsh breath. 'Well, that makes everything clear, doesn't it? For the last five years I've been living in a fool's paradise. It had occurred to me that you were waiting until she was eighteen before you got married, Daniel, but I was stupid enough to think that was just so that you could be free of family responsibilities. It never entered my head that you were waiting for her to be old enough to marry you.'

'I'll see you out,' Daniel said flatly.

'I'll find my own way out,' Barbara snapped. She turned and stared at Louise, her eyes sweeping down over the boyishly slender figure in jeans and an old sweater. 'You two are obviously made for each other —you're both of you as hard as iron and totally ruthless.' She gave Daniel a bitter smile. 'But watch out, Daniel. She's still very young. When she's older she's going to be a raving beauty, and when you're nearing fifty she'll still only be in her twenties, and the men will be all around her like flies around a jampot ... she'll break your heart, and if I'm still around I'll laugh until I'm sick!'

Daniel made no move as she walked out. Louise watched him quietly, anxiety in the depths of her blue eyes. He moved to the window and stood there, his hands in his pockets, his shoulders drooping.

'Unpleasant as she was,' he said huskily, 'there was truth in what she said. When I'm well into middle age, you'll still be a young girl. I must have been mad to suggest we got married.'

'Did you want to marry Barbara?' she asked in a controlled voice.

He shook his head.

'Are you certain, Daniel?'

He turned then, his face sardonic. 'Why on earth did you tell her those lies? Why, Louise?'

She felt her colour deepen. 'It shut her up,' she said, her mouth impish.

Daniel stared for a second, then his eyes filled with glinting amusement. 'You little witch ... she was right, you're capable of being ruthless.'

She walked over to him and slid her arms around him, leaning her head on his shoulder with a long sigh of content. 'You're mine,' she said softly. 'When I was eight years old you told me you were.'

'Did I?' His hand caressed her black hair gently. 'What a memory you've got, Louise!'

'I remember everything you've ever said to me,' she said.

His fingers played with a long strand of the silky hair. 'Why did you tell her you knew I'd been her lover?'

Her eyes closed against the stab of pain, but her voice was quite cool and showed nothing of it. 'I've never thought you were a monk, Daniel. You've been seeing Barbara for years, I guessed it was more than a friendship.'

'There have been others,' he said, almost as though he were confessing to her.

'You're thirty-five. What else could I expect?' she asked.

He sighed. 'We're running a terrible risk, darling. There are so many years between us, such a lot of life we haven't shared ...'

'Such a lot we have,' she said quietly. 'Most of mine, anyway. Could you know any woman as well as you do me?'

He laughed softly, kissing the top of her head. 'My own little Snow White ... no, that's true, but then it isn't me who is running the risk, darling. It's you. What if you meet another man later on? Someone nearer your own age?'

Louise moved away, lifting brilliant blue eyes to his face, her mouth teasing. 'Would you be a chivalrous knight and divorce me?'

Daniel's face altered, a glint in his eyes. 'Like hell I would! What I have, I keep.'

She put her hands on his shoulders, leaning back lightly, smiling at him. 'That's not the attitude of a gentleman.'

'Who said I was a gentleman?' he asked wryly. 'If I had any moral qualities at all, I'd never have got myself into this.'

She leaned forward very slowly, her eyes on the hard line of his mouth.

He caught her suddenly by the arms, holding her away from him, his face a mask. 'Listen to me, Louise ... I want you to promise me something.'

'What?' she asked cautiously, her instincts warning her.

'After we're married, give it six months,' he said flatly.

She frowned. 'Give what six months?'

He flushed darkly. 'Marriage,' he said carefully.

Her eyes searched his face, trying to read his feelings.

'Even six months isn't a fair trial,' he said, sighing. 'But at least it will give us a few clues. So, for the first six months, I want you to try just living with me. Nothing else.' His eyes were restless. 'No shared bedrooms. No consummation. Just being together.'

She studied him from beneath her lashes. 'A trial marriage without strings? Why?'

'If at the end of that time either of us wants out, we can break away without too much grief,' he said levelly. 'Once we've become lovers things could get very rough.'

'You said you would never divorce me,' she reminded him. 'Just a moment ago.'

'Not once you've been mine,' he said deeply. 'If I take you, I'll never let you go.'

Her heart plunged with passion and sweetness. She looked into the restless opalescent eyes and a curving smile of love touched her mouth.

'If that's what you want, Daniel,' she said softly.

'It's what I think we ought to do,' he replied flatly, 'for the sake of my conscience.'

Despite the strains of outside interference, the amazed, anxious telephone calls from friends and distant relations, the Vicar's harassed disbelief, the newspaper stories, somehow the relationship between them had been restored to something very like the way it had always been. Over the next few weeks they were together all the time, riding in the park, planning the wedding, listening to music in the evenings, and each day as it passed filled with a warm glow of content.

Louise returned, almost by instinct, to her jeans and shirts, only occasionally wearing her new adult dresses. Daniel, she sensed, was happier when she looked casually young. He treated her with the same warm, easy affection he had always given her, and never, by word or look, gave any hint of a deeper feeling. Ducky, watching them, seemed puzzled by the quiet tenor of their relationship.

Louise had ceased to provoke and arouse Daniel. The approaching date of their wedding laid a calming spell on her feelings. Laughing with him, in the evenings, she almost felt she had returned to earlier times, and she was in no hurry to change things.

She had chosen to be married in a very simple dress of ivory silk, the neckline high around her throat, buttoned with small pearls, curving down her bodice and nipping in the tiny waist, flowing out again gently to give her a smooth outline. The underskirts of stiffened lace and satin rustled as she walked around the bedroom before the ceremony. Ducky followed her, her mouth pinched with excitement. 'Keep still, cherub . . . it isn't hanging properly at the back.'

In the mirror the strange reflection eyed her. Under the full ivory lace veil brilliant blue eyes burned in a pale face. Her black hair was twined in a loose knot on her slender white neck, exposing the long white throat around which Daniel's wedding gift of a triple strand of pearls hung gleaming softly.

Will was giving her away. When she asked him, he had looked at her with bolt-eyed disbelief, shaking his head in horror. 'It's not my place,' he had muttered. 'I couldn't.'

'What other father have I ever had?' she had asked him softly.

His face had flushed and he had given her a long, loving look. Ducky had turned away to make a pot of tea, sniffing with her back to them.

'Mr Daniel wouldn't like it,' Will had protested, before giving in.

'I've already told him,' she said, laughing. 'He said it was a splendid idea.'

'The guests will be embarrassed,' Will said gruffly.

'You and Ducky and Daniel are my family,' she said simply. 'What do I care what anyone else thinks?'

His horror at the sight of morning dress had given her the giggles. 'Daniel wants it like this,' she said to him. 'You'll just have to grin and bear it for a few hours.'

Will looked, in fact, as if he had been born to it, his wiry figure erect in the formal clothes, his weathered face wooden beneath the top hat.

When Louise and Ducky came down to meet him, his face worked in visible emotion, his eyes running over the slender white figure as it approached.

'You look lovely, darling,' he said, clearing his throat.

Ducky, in a bright green dress and hat wreathed in lily of the valley, gave a cluck of irritation over his tie. 'What have you been doing to it? Leave you to yourself for five minutes and it looks like a rag!'

Somehow they were in the long white car and

Louise felt her throat tightening, her body quivering with a deep, nervous delight. Autumn had given the park at Queen's Dower a glowing radiance, the colours of the dying leaves shading from brown to flame, the wind blowing them in sheaves over the short grass.

She glanced back at the mellow warmth of the house, seeing it for the very last time as a child, her eyes touching it lovingly. When she saw it again she would see it as Daniel's wife, its mistress, and she felt as if the house itself were waiting for that moment, as she had waited, since she was eight years old.

The little village church was crowded. Everyone in the village was there. Except, Louise thought, walking down the aisle, possibly Barbara. There had been no sight or sound from her since the night she came to confront them. Rumour said she was selling her shop and leaving the district. The thought was an enormous relief.

Louise had known the church all her life. The familiar flint walls, irregular, grey, touched with slate-blue here and there, had a cosy look among the dark yew trees which surrounded it. Planted before Agincourt some of them, used by bowmen from the parish to make their bows when they went to fight in France, the ancient trees whispered in the autumn wind outside. Among the moss-grown gravestones lay the flat faded monument to a crusader. Familiar local names adorned many stones. Families tended to go on for generations here, some of them in the same trades.

Along the cream-washed walls of the little church the name Norfolk leapt out at her again and again. The family had lived and died at Queen's Dower for so long. These walls had been them come to be baptised, married and buried.

Heads craned to stare at her. The organ wheezily accompanied her slow procession towards Daniel. She kept her eyes fixed on his dark head, love like a furnace in her eyes.

He turned and their eyes met, the flame leaping between them, an act of acknowledgement, a promise.

Louise said her vows very clearly, her voice cool and distinct, without nervousness, without hesitation. She felt triumph so deep it was beyond expression. Daniel was more nervous, she sensed. He was very pale and his hands shook as he placed the ring on her finger. The air was filled with the scent of the flowers Mrs Blundell had arranged in huge masses around the altar. The chill of the stone church, inefficiently heated because the parish could not afford full central heating, mattered very little to her. The warmth of her delight kept her from noticing it.

Daniel said nothing at all in the car on the way back. From time to time he glanced at her and she smiled at him, her blue eyes alight with her feeling of belonging. When he helped her to alight at the house, Will and Ducky were already there, waiting. The reception was to be held in the state apartments, only ever used on these rare family occasions, and a small staff from the village had been installed to help with the catering.

Louise went into Ducky's arms first, kissing her. Then she turned to Will, and he said gruffly, 'Never looked so lovely, cherub, has she, Daniel?'

Daniel's eyes were brilliant, the opalescent flames consuming her. 'Never,' he said deeply, as if it cost him a good deal to speak at all.

Louise extended her hand, her fingers twining around his, and felt his grip tighten.

Slender, delicate, blue eyes vivid in her oval face, she stood at his side and welcomed the guests.

They had been carefully chosen. She and Daniel had drawn up the list in total unanimity. Most of the village was there, even the small children, and some of Daniel's friends. A few very distant relations had come obstinately, merely to be present, although none of them knew either her or Daniel except by sight and name.

She and Daniel began the dancing in the great hall, her slender body swaying in his arms, the silken swish of her skirts flaring around them as they danced.

When the others joined them, after a murmur of applause, Daniel looked down at her. 'Will's right,' he said softly. 'You've never looked more enchanting.'

'Getting married suits me,' she agreed, dimpling.

His arm tightened round her waist and he drew her closer, his lips against her forehead. She could hear his heart beating against her, and the knowledge that he was so nervous made her feel oddly grown up, as if she could understand him better than he could her. The thought was strange. Always, she had known that Daniel understood her, while she had only tried to understand him. Suddenly the position was reversed. It was a startling idea.

By the time the reception was over, she was very tired, drained by a long day of excitement and delight. As the last of the guests vanished she leaned against Daniel, a weary child, her head on his shoulder.

'Goodnight,' he said brusquely to Ducky and Will,

then lifted her into his arms, as if she were ten years old, and carried her up the stone stairs to the family apartment, her body heavy against him.

He laid her on her bed, slight and limp in the exquisite white dress, and she yawned. 'Help me get undressed, Daniel.'

'No, Louise,' he said harshly, spinning on his heel.

She heard the door slam and lay, smiling, on the bed. After a while she wearily got up and shed the beautiful silk and lace, hanging it carefully on the hangers Ducky had left in readiness.

Within ten minutes she was in bed, curled like a dormouse, her hand under her flushed cheek. Sleep washed over her without a pause.

CHAPTER EIGHT

THEY spent the week of their honeymoon at Queen's Dower, as they had planned, the days passing contentedly. They rode together in the park each day, fished in the stream, drove around the countryside, and the long hours they spent together had a warm radiance which somehow made the autumnal beauty of the park more glowing than usual. As a child, Louise had never been bored in Daniel's company, and knew that he was never bored by hers. She felt the same now, conscious of the deep bond between them which was stronger than iron, a shared understanding of each other which only years of living together could otherwise have brought to any other marriage. Their mutual love for the house and grounds was an unbreakable cement in that relationship. Each evening as they came back towards the house, either from a drive, or a walk around the park, each looked towards it with the same warm feeling, then looked at each other briefly, seeking the reflection of their own response in the other eyes.

Barbara, she thought, could never have shared that with him. Her mercenary, evaluating mind would have warped Daniel in time, hurt and angered him. Any woman who loved Daniel had to know and understand the depth of his roots in Queen's Dower. He was like one of the oaks in the park—all his life the deep tap root of his soul had gone down into the green land around the house, and he could not be parted from it or he would die.

The same applied to herself. Her intense love for the place was almost as deep as her love for Daniel. The two of them shared her heart. Sensitive to every flicker of expression in his face, she watched him as their marriage began, aware of every thought.

On the last evening of the honeymoon, he asked her quietly, 'What will you do when I've gone back to work?'

'Start running Queen's Dower,' she said.

He raised an eyebrow. 'Will Ducky like that?'

Louise smiled, her blue eyes dancing. 'I've talked it over with her. We're going to see how it works out. After all, there's more than enough work for both of us, and I can't see myself taking over Ducky's reign over the house, can you? She sees me as a sort of junior partner, here to learn my job, and that's fine with me.'

'So long as you're happy,' he said, his tone gentle.

'You know I am,' she said, thinking that this was what she had been training for all her life, this close weaving of her life with his, this total involvement with him.

'No regrets for art school?' he asked, tongue in cheek.

She pinched his hand. 'Only for the handsome art students I might have met.'

The smile he gave was slightly barbed. 'Well, if it doesn't work out, you can always go there later.'

'So I can,' she agreed, her lashes drooping.

Daniel watched her impudent, soft-flushed face with a wry tenderness. She looked up and they grinned at each other.

She found Ducky a hard taskmistress. Over the

years the routine of caring for the house had become settled and unchangeable. Ducky had only one way of doing everything, and she would not even consider any other way. Louise obediently began to fit herself into the pattern; following Ducky around, learning how to polish the ancient glowing oak panels, how to clean silver until it shone and reflected her own small face, how to scrub the soft rose tiles in the old kitchens. The million and one jobs which had to be done were performed by Ducky and her village helpers, but there was always some job which needed doing somewhere in the house.

'A good idea you learning it like this,' Ducky said to her, as they scrubbed the creamy stone which made the surround of the old windows. 'When I'm not here, I'll be glad to know the house is being looked after the right way.'

'You'll be here for ever and ever,' said Louise with the euphoria of youth, her eyes loving.

Ducky gave her a smiling, wry look. 'Nice of you to say so, but my rheumatism when it rains tell me otherwise.'

The blue eyes were sober at once. 'Don't, Ducky,' she said with deep uneasiness. 'Nothing must ever change.'

'Even you have changed,' said the warm voice. 'Some days you could be our little cherub. Other days you're suddenly a young woman, the mistress of Queen's Dower.'

'I haven't changed an inch,' Louise declared, pushing back a long strand of black hair with a wet hand.

'How horribly true!' Daniel's voice said in her ear, making her jump. She looked round, laughing, her small face smeared with the dust she had been removing from the window ledges.

He lifted her up, his hands tight around her slender waist. 'My God, you child,' he said mockingly, glancing down at her jeans and sweater. 'Look at you! I was going to take you out to dinner, but not looking like that.'

'Give me ten minutes,' she said eagerly. 'Ducky, do you mind finishing that, please?'

'You have a good time,' said Ducky, her eyes amused as Daniel dragged Louise towards their staircase.

After a long soak in a scented bubbling bath, Louise dressed in a rose-pink dress, piling her hair in a soft mass at the back of her head. Daniel surveyed her from head to foot when she joined him, his glance shifting from the smooth white shoulders to the tiny waist, then over the long, slender shapely legs.

'Turn round,' he commanded.

She twirled, her foot pointed like a ballet dancer, her skirts flying out.

'Very seductive,' he said drily.

She gave him a laughing glance, her long black lashes hiding the secretive gleam in the blue eyes, hearing the echo of a deeper emotion in his careful voice. She had been watching for weeks for some break in the wall with which he had surrounded himself since their marriage. She was in no hurry; they had all the time in the world. But she wanted nothing to go wrong between them again. They had got back the loving ease of their old relationship, and she was sure that time would slowly work the rest. Daniel had to be convinced that she was not too young to respond to him, too young to know what she was doing.

He took her to a small country hotel where they ate dinner by candlelight, talking quietly, completely at ease. When their eyes met a smile shot between them, an instinctive smile filled with the warmth of their feelings for each other. Louise was so aware of utter happiness that she was blithely gay as they drove home afterwards, singing under her breath, watching Daniel's long hard hands on the wheel with a peculiar inward flutter.

She made cocoa in the kitchen while he put the car away, and he came into the room to get his cup, leaning against the door, watching her as she neatly washed the saucepan and put it away.

'Ducky's making a good job of training you, I see,' he taunted, watching her delicate profile.

She grinned at him. 'She's a slave-driver!'

Childishly she took the skin off her cocoa with her finger and licked it, her small tongue flickering. Sipping the cocoa afterwards, she felt his eyes on her, and looked up, ready to smile. He was oddly expressionless, but his eyes were leaping.

She looked down, her heart thudding. Finishing the cocoa, she washed out the two cups and left them to drain, then moved to the door. Daniel still leaned there, his eyes on her. As she drew level she glanced up, her pulse beating at the base of her throat. Daniel drew her towards him silently and bent to kiss her.

She turned towards him eagerly, her face tilting, but the kiss was light and gentle, a brush over her lips which left her hungry for more.

She put her hands on his shoulders, smiling at him. 'Kiss me again, Daniel,' she whispered, her pink mouth curving with invitation.

'Go to bed, Louise,' he said huskily.

Her hands slid inward to grip the strong sides of his neck, her fingers caressing. She swayed forward and placed her mouth softly on his, her lips parting.

Daniel pushed her away almost violently. 'I said go to bed,' he snapped.

She felt her face burn. The rejection had been so abrupt, so harsh.

Without a word, she turned and walked to her own room. She only just had time to close the door before the tears came, and they went on for a long time.

The weeks slowly passed. Louise was kept very busy, running the house, helping Ducky, learning how to do things just as Ducky liked them done. Daniel remained a warm, friendly stranger, just beyond her, never coming closer than he had before. He treated her with the old loving gentleness of a brother to a sister. He occasionally took her out to dinner or to the cinema, but they never progressed beyond the unequal balance of a young girl to a man twice her age.

Louise made no attempt to change it; Daniel's harsh rejection had been too bitterly hurtful. She would never again try to show him her own feelings.

She believed now that Daniel had married her for a complicated strand of reasons. He had known instinctively that Barbara would never be suitable as mistress of Queen's Dower. He had known equally surely that Louise would always love the house as he did. And his long affection for her had predisposed him to want to hold her, although he felt a great deal of misgivings about marrying someone so much younger than himself.

She knew he found her attractive—he had proved

it by his jealousy in the past. She knew he loved her, but perhaps, she felt sadly, his love was still that of an older brother for a child, and he was refusing to grant her the status of womanhood because he found his own attraction towards her somehow unacceptable.

One early winter evening she was riding in the park, her slender body warmly clad in a thick white sweater and jodhpurs, when she saw a man in the drive, a camera around his neck, taking a photograph of Queen's Dower.

The tourists were only permitted in the grounds during the summer. Quietly Louise rode up to him and reined, looking down at him. He was a man approaching thirty, she guessed, wearing an extremely unusual and elegant suit in a bronze shade which complemented his thick brown hair and dark eyes.

'I'm sorry,' she said politely, 'but I'm afraid the house and grounds are shut during the winter months. You're trespassing.'

He gave her a casual grin which gave charm to his strong face. 'So I saw by the noticeboard as I came through the gates. Do you keep bloodhounds, or will the flunkeys throw me out?'

Somehow the question was delivered so pleasantly it fell short of insolence, and she laughed. 'Neither,' she admitted. 'I'll just ask you to go, if you don't mind. This is a home, not just a public showplace.'

He ran a considering eye over Velvet's sleek coat, the obvious air of birth and breeding which the animal carried, then lifted it to survey Louise in an almost identical fashion, his dark eyes flashing over her slender, graceful body.

'Your home?' he asked easily.

'Yes,' she said, her face amused.

'Is your name Norfolk?' he pressed.

'Louise Norfolk,' she agreed, suddenly revealing the dimple in the smooth skin of her cheek which only came when she was very amused.

'Louise ...' He murmured the name thoughtfully. 'That's not a family name.'

She lifted an eyebrow, curious.

He grinned at her. 'I'm a Norfolk, too ... one of your American cousins. My great-grandfather left for America in the nineteenth century. He was the fourth son of the fellow who owned Queen's Dower, then. Roger, his name was ... I'm named after his father, Garnon.'

'Garnon Norfolk?' Louise exclaimed, astonished. 'His portrait hangs in the hall.'

'Sure does,' the man nodded. 'I've been hearing about Queen's Dower since I was old enough to listen. We've got a family tree in our bible at home, the greatest treasure in the house.'

Louise was studying him curiously. 'Come to think of it,' she said, 'you do have a look of Garnon Norfolk ... the colouring is the same, and he had the same nose.'

He felt his nose wryly. 'Enormous, isn't it? I curse the day he left it with me.'

She giggled. 'You must come up to the house and look around, Mr Norfolk.'

'I was hoping you would say that,' he grinned. 'And the name is Garnon, Louise.'

She walked Velvet slowly towards the house while he strolled beside her, telling her about the years during which he had grown up hearing of Queen's Dower. 'My father visited it when he was a young man, but somehow I never got around to it until now. I was sure sore when I got over here and found the house was closed to visitors.'

'It always is in winter,' Louise told him. 'We live here still, you know.'

'Damned lucky you are, too,' he said, staring up at the house with rapt delight. 'My God, it's beautiful!'

'Yes,' Louise agreed, 'very beautiful.' She watched him, touched by his expression. His face reflected the amazement, the pleasure she still felt whenever she saw the warm red brick and peaceful atmosphere of the house.

'Come on in,' she invited, slipping off Velvet's back, leading her into the stables. Will came out and stared at the stranger, his eyes shrewd.

Louise looked at him with a smile. 'Will, this is Garnon Norfolk. Garnon, this is Will, who looks after the house with us.'

Will slowly took the hand offered to him, staring closely at the other man. He made a wry face. 'I thought I'd seen that face somewhere before,' he said. 'It's the nose.'

'Oh, good grief, my nose!' sighed Garnon disconsolately.

'It's your pedigree,' Louise said, laughing. 'Come in and take a look at the donor of it.'

In the great hall he stood entranced, staring around in the gathering dusky light. Louise flicked on the electric lights so that he could see better. He stood in front of the rather dull portrait of his ancestor, studying the heavy, obstinate face with a grimace.

'All beef and beer, Daniel calls him,' she said, laughing.

'Well, thanks for recognising me,' Garnon commented.

She smiled at him. 'Oh, only the nose ... a very commanding nose, you must admit.'

It was as fleshless as an eagle's beak in the wide Victorian face. On Garnon it somehow looked stronger, more dominant.

Louise led him round the hall, pointing out family relics which he eyed with fascination. 'My mother would have loved this,' he said. She glanced at him, picking up the regret in his tone, and he said quietly, 'She died a few years back. Always wanted to see the house, but it was too expensive a trip, I guess.'

'I'm sorry,' she said. 'And your father?'

'Oh, he's fine,' Garnon told her. 'It was his idea I came this time. He's keen for me to see just what we lost when we went to the States. Mind you, we got quite a lot in exchange.'

'What do you do for a living?' she asked curiously, leading him up to the other public rooms.

'I'm in electronics,' he said.

He followed her around the rooms, asking questions, staring, showing great interest in everything. 'Somehow I didn't expect it to be so fantastic,' he said. 'My dad's stories were just that bit too good to be true, but I guess they were all true, after all. This house is a perfect jewel.'

She led him into her own rooms and offered him a drink. 'I'd ask you to stay to dinner, but my husband is taking me out tonight,' she said.

He stared at her, his jaw dropping. 'Husband?' His voice sounded incredulous.

She flushed, seeing his glance at her hand, and held it out, a little defiantly, so that the gold band and the

sapphire engagement ring Daniel had placed there
could sparkle in the light.

'Yes, I'm Mrs Norfolk,' she admitted shyly. 'Daniel
Norfolk is my husband. As you said, Louise isn't a
family name.'

Garnon was flushed. 'I'm sorry, I didn't intend to
be rude. It's just that I thought you must be his kid
daughter ... you look so damned young.' And his
eyes ran over her jodhpurs and slender figure again
with the same disbelieving light.

She looked away, her face suddenly cool and
haughty. 'You must stay and meet Daniel when he
come back from work,' she said politely, her face
averted.

They sat down, sipping their drinks, and talked for
half an hour, while the darkness of the winter night
filled the park with a rushing wind and the whispering
of the old trees.

'It must be terrific to live here,' Garnon commented. 'But a bit unreal.'

'It's very real to me,' she assured him, smiling

'How long have you lived here?' he asked. 'When
did you get married?'

'I've lived here since I was five,' she told him. 'But
I only married Daniel a few months ago.'

'How come you lived here?' he asked.

She explained, and he stared at her curiously, his
dark eyes inspecting her again, taking in the delicate
beauty of her oval face, the sleek black hair and
gentle mouth.

Suddenly the telephone began to shrill. Louise
answered it, and was surprised to hear Daniel's voice.
'I'm sorry, darling, but I've got to stay in Bristol to-

night. A Japanese buyer is in town and I have to take him to dinner. I'll make it up to you tomorrow, I promise.'

'Oh, what a pity,' she said, deeply disappointed. 'Never mind ...'

'I must rush,' he said quickly. 'I'll see you later. Don't wait up for me, I may be late.'

He had gone before she could tell him about Garnon, and she replaced the receiver with a sigh. Turning, she smiled at him. 'I'm so sorry, I'm afraid that was my husband. Business has snatched him off, so no dinner for me tonight, and I won't be able to introduce you.'

'Well, that's a shame,' Garnon said thoughtfully. 'You've been so kind, showing me around the house. Will you let me take you out to dinner as a grateful gesture? I'm leaving tomorrow, so I won't be able to show my gratitude some other time, or I would have loved to meet your husband.'

She hesitated, unsure whether to accept or not. Daniel's failure to come home had left her evening quite free, it was true, and she had been looking forward to dinner somewhere.

'Please,' Garnon pleaded. 'There's a lot more I want to hear about the house.'

She capitulated, smiling. 'You're very kind. Thank you, I would very much enjoy having dinner with you.'

'My hotel in Bristol does a good meal,' he said.

'That sounds fine,' she nodded. 'Will you excuse me while I change?'

He nodded, rising as she left the room. His manners were excellent, she thought, and he was a very nice man. Daniel would be unlikely to object. After all, Garnon was a member of the family, even if a remote one.

She flicked through her dresses doubtfully, and on an impulse chose the glimmering blue one which she had last worn at the dance to which she had gone with Sally and Peter. She had not worn it since, and it seemed a good opportunity.

When she emerged in it about fifteen minutes later, Garnon rose, openly staring, his eyes clearly filled with surprise.

He whistled softly. 'Now I believe you're Mrs Norfolk,' he said, smiling at her.

She called in to explain to Ducky where she was going, and to say that Daniel would not be home until much later. Ducky looked stiffly disapproving, rather coldly shaking hands with the American.

In the car as they drove to Bristol, Garnon said, his voice filled with wry amusement. 'I guess the lady didn't take to me.'

'Oh, Ducky's wonderful once she gets to know you,' she assured him.

'But she doesn't approve of you going out with strange Americans?' he asked.

She laughed. 'Ducky has a code she lives by, and the rules are unbreakable.'

'Will your husband mind?' he asked, glancing at her.

She flushed. 'I'm sure he won't.' But suddenly she wasn't so sure. Ducky's grim glances had had their effect. Louise was getting cold feet.

Garnon's hotel was sited in the centre of Bristol. As they drove through the confusing maze of one-way streets which made traffic so impossible if one was a stranger, they passed the hotel without noticing it, and Garnon groaned. 'I guess that's the tenth time I've missed the place since I arrived ... I've got no bump of locality.' He reversed into an alley and they approached the hotel again, slowing to turn into the underground car park.

As they did, Louise casually glanced along the pavement and with a shock saw Daniel, his dark head glinting in the light from the hotel. He was standing with Barbara just beside the entrance. As Louise stared, her heart sick with jealousy, she saw Barbara lean forward and kiss him on the mouth, and her last glimpse of them was as Daniel's hands came up to catch hold of her.

Garnon parked and turned towards her, swinging his key ring from his finger. 'Well, here we are,' he said lightly, then stared at her, 'Say, what's wrong? You're as white as a ghost.'

She was trembling, her body chilled. 'I'm fine,' she said huskily.

'The devil you are,' Garnon muttered, taking her shoulders and turning her towards him. 'What is it, honey?'

The soft concern of his voice brought the tears rushing into her eyes. She helplessly leant against his shoulder and cried, and he put his arms around her, patting her back.

When she had stopped crying she sat up, wiping her nose and face with a childlike dignity on the handkerchief he provided. 'I'm sorry,' she said faintly.

'Now, what was that all about?' he asked kindly. 'Come on, two heads are better than one, and I should know. I've had two for years.'

She giggled weakly at the old joke. 'I can't talk

about it,' she said after a moment. 'Please, forget it ...
I'm all right now.'

'You look terrible,' he said. 'And I'm being very
kind when I say that.'

She smiled at him, her blue eyes enormous in her
white face. 'You are very kind,' she said softly. 'Thank
you.'

He considered her soberly. 'Okay, you don't want
to talk about it. So let's go into the hotel. You go
to the powder room and put the sparkle back in your
eyes, then we'll have dinner ... when a girl's been
crying, champagne is always very cheering.'

In the cloakroom Louise washed slowly, then
applied fresh make-up with hands that shook. Daniel
had lied to her. He had met Barbara tonight, not
some Japanese. And they had made love. She felt sick
misery in her stomach. Oh, God, she thought ... I
can't live with him and watch him lie to me and go
off with her in secret.

Barbara had said he would come back to her. They
had been lovers for years.

How many other women had there been in secret?
she thought. All those years of her childhood he had
kept them all away from Queen's Dower to hide them
from her. What strange, bizarre thinking made him
want both herself and these others, the women like
Barbara, beautiful and acquisitive, whom he did not
love, but whom he went on seeing?

She stared at herself in the mirror. The bright lights
of the little room made her look younger, more delicate, more frail than ever. She suddenly saw herself as
Daniel's possession, like Queen's Dower, something
he wanted to own, something he cherished. She was
like one of the fragile objects in the glass cases. She

belonged at Queen's Dower—he had often told her so. He had said she had to stay there. Daniel would not let her go; he was deeply possessive by instinct.

But although he was determined to own her, he did not regard her as a woman at all, only as the child he had called his little Snow White, a precious thing to be kept in a crystal case and never touched.

Her heart froze at the thought. A marriage which was no marriage, a love which was no true love ... could she bear to accept that?

Slowly she rejoined Garnon, who studied her, his mouth compassionate. 'Come on, honey,' he said. 'Champagne!'

The meal was excellent, the service attentive— Louise was amused to realise that Garnon's American accent was the cause for that. The waiters hovered eagerly as he poured her champagne, insisting that she drink it.

She drank deliberately, needing the flush and release of the wine in her blood. Garnon watched, amused. 'Whoa!' he said, after her third glass. 'Your head isn't quite straight any more, honey.'

'Good,' she said, laughing, her blue eyes brilliant in her flushed face. 'You've got two heads now, Garnon, even though you had one before!'

He laughed, his eyes kind. 'I think some black coffee would be the answer to that,' he said.

'No black coffee,' she said decisively. 'I want to fly!'

'We can dance,' he suggested. 'They have dancing here later on ... after the black coffee.'

Louise allowed him to get her some black coffee, which she sipped distastefully, then they sat at their table while the floor was cleared and the dancing started. The small band played with a strong beat which filled the room. Garnon led Louise on to the floor and grinned as she slid into his arms.

'You a good dancer, Louise?'

'You tell me?' she asked, her eyes teasing.

He looked down at her oddly. 'My God, you're beautiful,' he said suddenly. 'You're positively ravishing!'

'But totally unravished,' she said with a flicker of her lashes over wild blue eyes.

Garnon made no response, his eyes narrowing as he stared down at her. They danced together well. She was wrapped in her own web of comfort, humming under her breath, the champagne flowing in her veins, the rhythm of the music in her head.

She lost all sense of time. In between dances she persuaded Garnon to buy her a bubbling confection filled with fruit, the ingredients of which she never discovered. It bolstered the effect of the champagne, although Garnon clicked his tongue over it.

'I need it,' she said, briefly very grave.

'Yeah, I guess you do, honey,' he agreed gently, and watched her drink it with a thoughtful face.

'Well, Cinderella, it's midnight,' he said at last. 'Time for the pumpkin, I guess.'

'I don't want to go home,' she protested, her lower lip trembling.

He led her from the room, an arm around her waist. In the lift she suddenly began to cry again, silently, slowly, as though the tears stole down her face in secret.

Garnon pushed her head into his shoulder, his face grim over the top of her dark head. She let him put her into his car, and felt the cool of the night air on her face as they came up into the street. On the drive home she cried without stopping. At last Garnon stopped the car on a grass verge and turned and pulled her straight into his arms, cuddling her like a sad child.

'You've got to tell someone what's eating you, honey,' he said against her ear. 'Get it off your chest.'

Somehow she told him, her voice breaking, and he listened without interruption, his hand stroking her black head.

When she was quiet, her tears ended too, he said quietly, 'Now, I think you're jumping to conclusions here, Louise. Say you did see your husband with this other woman. There could be a dozen explanations for that. Wait until you hear his side of the story before you break your little heart over it.'

'He doesn't want me,' she said huskily, her cheeks hot. 'If he did he would have made love to me by now.'

Garnon looked down at her head and put a hand under her chin. 'Any man who looked at you would want you, Louise,' he said softly. 'You're a very desirable girl.'

Her eyes shyly met his, then looked away.

'Now, let's get you home,' he said, 'before I lose my head and scare you to death. And if I were you, I'd do something about those tear-stains before you get in ... I don't want my long-lost cousin punching me on the nose!'

She obeyed him as he drove the rest of the way to Queen's Dower. By the time they had driven up the dark winding drive to the house, she was restored to her former smooth look, her face calm. Garnon parked and turned towards her, putting a hand under her chin to inspect her.

'As I said,' he told her slowly, 'you're a very desirable girl, even when you're covered in tears ... like this, you're breathtaking.'

Louise smiled at him and leaned forward to kiss him gratefully. His arms slid round her and he pulled her closer, his mouth deepening the kiss very gently, persuasively, without alarming her.

Behind him his door opened abruptly. Louise heard Daniel's furious, biting voice, felt Garnon dragged back from her. Her eyes alarmed, she jumped out of the car herself just in time to see Daniel pulling Garnon out, a hand on his collar.

'Daniel, don't!' she cried, running round towards them.

Daniel's face was contorted with rage, as Garnon and he faced each other like enemies. Louise stood between them, facing Daniel coldly.

'Leave him alone,' she said with ice in her voice.

The opalescent eyes stared at her, narrowed on her face. There was a long silence.

'I kissed him first,' she said deliberately. 'And I wanted him to kiss me back.'

Daniel took a long breath, then turned on his heel and walked away.

Louise shivered, feeling sick. Garnon whistled under his breath. 'Honey, that wasn't wise.'

She turned and extended a hand. 'Thank you, Garnon, for the dinner and the kindness. Have a nice trip back to the States.'

'Will you be all right?' he asked her anxiously. 'That husband of yours isn't going to be easy to handle.'

'Daniel wouldn't hurt me,' she said flatly. 'I told you, I'm one of his cherished possessions.'

'One he doesn't like to see in another man's hands,' Garnon said pointedly. 'Honey, he was ready to kill me. I've seen that look in a man's eyes before and it means murder.'

'He won't hurt me,' she said calmly. 'Goodbye, Garnon.'

She watched him reluctantly drive away, then she walked into the house. Ducky was waiting, a sharpness to her mouth. Louise looked at her without speaking and went up the private stairs, sensing Ducky's stunned incredulity as she walked away. This time Ducky had to stay out of it. Louise felt very old as she went up the stairs. Tonight she had finally grown up, and the sensation was not happy.

CHAPTER NINE

When she passed through the door into their own rooms, she heard Daniel moving about in the sitting-room. She walked along the corridor stiffly, her head erect. As she passed the door of the room, he swung, facing her, a glass of whisky in his hand. 'Come in here,' he said tersely, swallowing the whisky as if he needed it.

Louise ignored him, walking very fast to her own room. Bolting the door, she began to undress, unzipping the blue dress and allowing the shimmering material to slide away from her into a little heap on the floor.

Daniel spoke sharply outside the door. 'Come out of there, Louise! We're going to talk, whether you like it or not.'

She slowly took off all her other clothes, and put on a cream silk wrap with wide lapels which left a tantalising plunge of soft skin visible, tying the belt around her waist. Slowly she brushed her hair, staring at herself in the mirror, hearing Daniel's angry voice get angrier as he hammered on the door. Walking across the room, she carefully hung up her blue dress, then threw her discarded underclothes into a linen basket in the corner of the room.

Daniel was almost hoarse with temper by now. 'My God, I'll smash this door down if you don't come out!' he shouted, thudding his fist on the door.

She opened the door and they confronted each

other. Beneath the brushed, glossy black hair her small face was chill. 'I have nothing to say to you, Daniel,' she told him, turning towards the bathroom.

'Don't you dare to speak to me like that!' he snarled, grabbing her arm and whirling her round to face him. 'What the hell's got into you? Have you gone mad?'

'Let go of me,' she said, her voice frigid.

He stared down at her, his eyes leaping with rage. 'I suppose you've had a heady taste of the power you can have over men tonight,' he said in a low, thickened tone. 'This American came here, took one look and fell like a brick wall, did he? Well, I'm not putting up with it. You're my wife.'

'You're my husband,' she flung back bitterly.

His face reflected bewilderment and irritation. 'What the hell is that supposed to convey?'

'Garnon took me to dinner in Bristol,' she said coldly. 'As we drove past the hotel, you came out ... with Barbara, who kissed you.'

A flush mounted in his face, yet oddly he seemed to relax, some of the violent tension going out of his muscles. His blue-green eyes narrowed consideringly on her cold face. After a long pause he said huskily, 'So that's it.'

Burning with humiliation suddenly, Louise pulled out of his grip and walked into the bathroom, slamming the door behind herself. Slowly she washed and cleaned her teeth. She took her time, expecting to find him still out there when she opened the door, but when she eventually came out there was no sign of him.

Although she was so angry, disappointment made her sick. Gritting her teeth, she walked into her bedroom and halted, her heart leaping, seeing him stand there, having changed into his dressing-gown, a present she had given him last Christmas, thick towelling in blue and white stripes.

She gave him one look, then looked away. 'There's no more to be said between us, Daniel,' she said. 'I want an annulment. I'm not sharing you with Barbara. I'm leaving you tomorrow.'

He watched her, his face unreadable. 'I'll take it point by point,' he said flatly. 'Number one, I had dinner with a Japanese buyer tonight. You can check with the damned hotel, if you refuse to believe me. It was sheer misfortune that Barbara happened to be staying at the place. She's on her way to Australia, apparently; she leaves next week. She made it impossible for me to ignore her, so she joined myself and the Japanese for a drink, then I walked her out to get a taxi. She was going to visit friends. When she'd gone, I drove home. Early. I wanted to get back to you.'

Colour flowed into her cheeks and her eyes fell. 'Oh,' she whispered, 'I'm sorry. I ... I leapt to conclusions ...'

'I haven't seen her since our wedding, and I doubt if I'll ever see her again,' he said levelly. 'As to an annulment, the answer is no ... you won't be leaving me, tomorrow or any other day.'

'Suppose I want to go?' she asked, her heart leaping wildly.

'You silly, jealous little fool,' he muttered thickly, suddenly moving towards her. 'You'd die if you walked outside these gates.'

'Let me go,' she moaned as his arms came round

her, pushing him away. 'I won't be kept under glass all my life.'

'What are you babbling about now?' he asked with rough amusement, lifting her struggling off her feet and up into his arms.

'You want me like one of those precious family relics in the hall, to look at, not to touch,' she cried wildly, her blue eyes filling with tears.

For a moment Daniel looked down into her face, an odd twisted smile on his mouth, then he flung her across the bed and fell beside her, threading his hands through her long hair, hurting her, pulling her head back with a jerk, tilting it up to him.

'You don't know what the hell you're talking about, my darling,' he said in grim sarcasm. 'You're so damned young. I've been waiting for four years for you to grow up, but you've taken your time about it . . .'

The blue eyes widened until the soft white skin was stretched in disbelief.

He held her eyes, lowering his head, and her heart began a wild crescendo of passion as his mouth came down on hers, the heat and hunger of his kiss sending the blood pumping violently around her body. Her lips parted involuntarily, the pressure of the hard male mouth sending her abruptly out of all control, her long-denied need of him fuelled by the first touch, blazing with a response which was untrammelled. The slender, silk-clad body clung to him, the slight arms twining round his neck, and she gave a low, muffled groan of hunger under his exploring mouth.

He reluctantly freed his mouth and lifted his head, his opalescent eyes glittering, running possessively over the small, flushed, intensely aroused face below him. 'I ought to beat you for letting a total stranger kiss you like that. You did it deliberately just to give me hell, didn't you, Louise? When will you grow up? How could you believe I would lie and cheat you like that?'

'It hurt to see you with her,' she whispered shakily.

'You didn't have to go straight into another man's arms,' he said fiercely. 'Do you know how close I came to murder?'

'You walked away,' she said incredulously, staring at him.

'It was either that or kill one of you,' he said tautly. 'I walked away to keep my temper before I did something I might regret. I know you too well to have suspected you'd done more than let him kiss you, but ...' He broke off, running his hands through the silvered black hair. 'My God, when will you realise I'm insanely in love with you, you idiotic child? I've been having the devil's own time of it for weeks keeping my own hands off you, then I see you in another man's arms ... I could have gone mad!'

Her heart was racing so fiercely she was breathless. She gazed at him incredulously. 'Daniel!' Her love was so immense the sound of his name was filled with it.

He stared down, reading the restless vulnerable young face with eyes that ate her. 'I first knew how I felt about you on your fourteenth birthday,' he said abruptly, his mouth grim. 'I came into your room with your birthday present. You remember that new saddle I bought you?'

'You left it on the end of my bed while I was asleep,' she said with a happy smile.

'You were fast asleep when I came in,' he said thickly. 'You'd been excited about your birthday. You always slept restlessly when you were excited, and you'd kicked off all your bedclothes ... I looked down at you with a grin, then suddenly it hit me, like a tidal wave. You were wearing a ridiculous short nightie, some blue nylon thing ... I found myself looking at you and feeling this terrible hunger. I threw down the saddle and cleared out, hating myself. I walked around the garden for hours, telling myself it was a brief madness. When you came down to breakfast in your jodhpurs you looked a child again, and I breathed easier. I still felt sick whenever I remembered the way I'd felt, but I thought it was just a touch of lunacy.'

Louise watched him gravely, reading the scratched lines of pain in his hard face.

'Sometimes I could forget it entirely for months,' he said flatly. 'Then something would send it flashing back and I'd be in hell. I was furious with myself, but I couldn't stop it. My sweet, fragile little Snow White ... I loathed myself, but I couldn't stop wanting you. It got worse and worse. I began dreaming about you. I'd wake up feeling an intense aching agony. My only consolation was that you obviously had no idea at all ... you were still just a child.'

She ran the soft palms of her small hands over his taut face, feeling the tight muscles under her skin. 'Darling!'

He turned his head and kissed one palm adoringly. 'Then there was that day at the fair. You know how I reacted then. I was so jealous I almost blew my skull.'

She looked at him tenderly and he gave her a dark glance.

'That was when you saw how I felt, wasn't it? I knew you'd begun to realise you could torment me. You were drunk with adolescent power, enjoying the ability to tease and tantalise me.'

'No,' she protested. 'I loved you. When I came back from school I thought you were waiting for me. I thought it was all going to be so simple. We loved each other, I thought. Then you came with Barbara and you were so offhand and cold. I was hurt and bewildered.'

'So you used young Blare to get back at me,' he said harshly. 'You were so set on hurting me that you never noticed how he felt, but I did, oh, God, I did. I was terrified. He was only a boy, but he felt like a man, and I was awake half the night while he was here, wondering how I was going to stave off the disaster I was afraid might happen if he ever got out of control.'

'Poor Peter,' she said sadly, 'I treated him very badly.'

'You did,' Daniel agreed curtly. 'You used him as a weapon against me without ever considering what you were doing to him. I hated watching it, partly because it showed how immature you still were ... you were still just a child, and I was only too aware that we weren't evenly matched. That's why I kept you at arms' length—I had to. My self-control was beginning to slip badly whenever we were alone. You'd learnt how to get under my skin very quickly, you little witch. Several times you tantalised me into losing my head.'

She lowered her eyes, suddenly grave. 'Yet you spent my first night home with Barbara.'

He laughed curtly. 'No, my darling. I walked miles

that bloody night. I had to wear myself out before I came back into the house. Do you think I found it easy to sleep with you just a few rooms away from me?'

She smiled brilliantly at him, her heart singing. 'Barbara told me you were her lover and you admitted it.'

He grimaced. 'There was a time,' he admitted grimly. 'When I first realised how I was beginning to want you. I tried to put you out of my head. Barbara was a very inviting and experienced female, and I wanted to forget you, but somehow it never worked.'

Louise sighed with relief. 'Why have you been so cold to me since we were married, then?' she asked, sliding her fingers into his hair, ruffling it into shining dark peaks.

'I was waiting for you to know your own mind,' he said flatly. 'I was aware that you thought you loved me—your response when I kissed you told me that you were attracted to me. But the terrified way you ran from young Blare showed me how little ready for marriage you were.'

She looked at him through her dark lashes, her mouth curving. 'You darling idiot!' she whispered. 'Do you really think I'd have run from you?'

Daniel caught his breath, staring down into her eyes. 'Louise,' he said hoarsely. 'Dearest ... I'll try to be gentle, but I'm afraid I'll lose control. I've needed you for so long. If I frighten you or hurt you, stop me ...'

She slid her arms around his neck, her eyes a brilliant, melting blue. 'Take what's been yours since I was eight years old, Daniel,' she whispered.

'You siren,' he muttered, burying his face in the

warm white throat, his mouth sliding over her skin hungrily. 'Oh, God, I want you ...'

'Daniel,' she moaned, pulling his head round towards her. Her arms tightened round his neck and then she gave a smothered gasp of delight and astonishment as the kiss deepened beyond anything she had ever experienced before, an unleashed demand in the hard possession of his lips which amounted almost to savagery, but a violence sweetened by love, softened by tenderness.

His hand slid beneath the cream silk, heating her warm skin, caressing and stroking over her. She could feel the tremble in the long fingers, the deep need, and her own passion flared to meet it.

His hands curved over the small, high breasts, leaving her shaking physically and mentally shattered by the sensations he was arousing. 'If I'm frightening you, tell me,' he whispered jerkily.

'Love me,' she moaned, her eyes shut. 'I want to belong to you.'

He untied the belt clumsily and her wrap fell open. She heard the fierce, ragged intake of his breath, heard his chest beating harshly, and her deep knowledge of him told her that he was trying to control his own feelings. The tension surrounding him was like a magnetic field. His eyes roved over the slight, white body as if he could hardly bear to stop staring at her.

Burning with sensual awareness, she pulled his dressing gown open and threw herself against him, clinging, kissing his shoulders, her hands digging into his skin. 'Take me, Daniel.'

Pleasure and pain combined in a wild consummation, her slender body fire in his arms, surrendering so naturally, with such ardent yearning hunger, that he completely forgot her delicate youth and his fear of frightening her, taking her as passionately as she offered herself, his possession of her without limit, boundless.

'You astounding child,' he groaned, kissing her afterwards. 'Oh, the time I've wasted ... the months ... how could I guess you would want me like this?'

'I love you,' she whispered, her soft mouth crushed and bruised during the tempest of his lovemaking, but smiling, content. 'I've always loved you, I always will.'

'I gambled on that,' Daniel said with a sigh. 'When I married you, I did it knowing what a risk I took, but hoping against hope that the way you seemed to feel would grow into an adult feeling. After young Blare I knew I had to lock you to me if I could, despite my own fear that I was cradle-snatching.'

'You should have done this that first night,' she said, her eyes teasing. 'I wanted it.'

'Do you think I didn't? When you invited me to take off your wedding dress I was half crazy. I had to get out of that room before I went quite mad.'

Louise sighed, lying against him, totally cradled, totally secure. 'It's always been you, all my life. There could never be another man.'

'There'd better not be,' he said flatly. 'You narrowly escaped being strangled tonight. I walked away from that car with murder in my heart.'

'Garnon said that,' she observed thoughtfully.

'Ah, our American friend,' he drawled. 'If I'm going to have to knock his teeth down his throat, you'd better tell me all about him.'

She laughed, her eyes slanting up at him. 'He's a Norfolk,' she told him. 'And he's flying back to the

States tomorrow.'

'Escaping vengeance by the skin of his teeth,' said Daniel, not altogether humorously.

'He was very kind and sweet to me,' she said softly.

Daniel's eyes were menacing. 'Careful, Louise!'

'After I saw you with Barbara I cried, and he comforted me.'

'I saw some of his brand of comfort, and I didn't like it,' he snarled.

'He said I was being silly,' she murmured very softly. 'That any man would find me desirable.'

Daniel took her neck between his two hands, his eyes glinting. 'Stop tormenting me, you little witch!'

'I'm sorry,' she said, her smile inviting.

He ran his hands down over her naked shoulders and let them curve desirously over the slender, sleek white body. 'Show me how sorry,' he said huskily. 'I've got an insatiable appetite for the taste of that little mouth of yours ...'

She lifted her mouth, her arms curving round his neck.

They woke astoundingly early, the first dawn chorus muffled in the winter morning air. Louise forgot for a second or two and stared round at Daniel's head on the pillow beside her, then a glow of radiant happiness came into her blue eyes, and she sat up on her elbow, one hand lightly brushing over his sleeping face. He groaned, his eyes reluctantly opening, and she saw his unguarded features at he looked at her. For just a second there was agony, incredulity, then a slow passion and remembering ... He reached out an arm and pulled her down against him, covering her with kisses.

'Let's ride,' she said, when the first onslaught had passed, her cheek against him.

'I have a much better idea,' Daniel muttered, his hands seeking out the warm curves of the slender body in his arm.

'I want to ride in the park,' she said, although her senses awoke and tingled under his fingers. 'I want to tell the house.'

Daniel gave a shout of laughter. 'You baby!'

She pinched him. 'We must,' she insisted. 'I want to ride back to Queen's Dower with you for breakfast, the way we always did, and everything will be perfect.'

His mouth was burning on her skin. 'Do you have to be told what I want to do?' he asked her huskily. 'I was never able to bear the idea of any other man teaching you what love was all about ... I had to do it. Do you remember asking me to teach you? You said it so artlessly, and you could have had no notion what it did to my pulses ... I was so tempted I could have screamed.'

She looked at him through her lashes, suddenly blushing hotly. 'It wasn't altogether artless,' she whispered.

His brows rose. 'What?'

'I was trying to give you a hint,' she confessed, her mouth half smiling, half grave. 'But I lost my nerve when you went so quiet. I though you might be furious with me. I was overcome with shame at being so ... so ...'

'Wanton?' he suggested, tongue in cheek.

'Beast!' she laughed, pummelling him.

He suddenly picked her up and dropped her out of the bed. Naked, startled, she stared at him. 'Get dressed,' he said, grinning. 'Let's have that precious ride of yours and tell the house.'

Queen's Dower in the grey winter light was a hard outline of red brick, the bare trees in the park mere shadows. They rode slowly over the turf and turned to look back as the pale sun slowly rose and brought the house to life, gilding the windows and tracing every graceful line of the building. Daniel sat on his gelding, his hard lean body casual, staring at his home with a contented mouth. Louise edged Velvet closer, her slender leg brushing against his, and he turned his head to glance down at her. Between the flowing, windblown black hair her oval face was wild with emotion, her blue eyes alight. 'I love you,' she said intensely.

He gave her a passionate glance, then laughed mockingly. 'Now she tells me, where I can't do a damn thing about it. To hell with breakfast, my darling ... let's go back to bed!'

ROMANCE

Variety is the spice of romance

Each month, Mills & Boon publish new romances. New stories about people falling in love. A world of variety in romance—from the best writers in the romantic world. Choose from these titles in December.

FOR ADULTS ONLY Charlotte Lamb
FLIGHT TO PASSION Flora Kidd
DOLPHINS FOR LUCK Peggy Nicholson
NO HOLDS BARRED Jessica Steele
A CHANGE OF HEART Sandra Field
THE DEVIL'S PAWN Yvonne Whittal
ONE LAST DANCE Claire Harrison
TROPICAL EDEN Kerry Allyne
HEIDELBERG WEDDING Betty Neels
LOVERS' KNOT Marjorie Lewty
RAGE Amanda Carpenter
BRIDE BY CONTRACT Margaret Rome

On sale where you buy paperbacks. If you require further information or have any difficulty obtaining them, write to: Mills & Boon Reader Service, PO Box 236, Thornton Road, Croydon, Surrey CR9 3RU, England.

Mills & Boon
the rose of romance

Best Seller Romances

Romances you have loved

Mills & Boon Best Seller Romances are the love stories that have proved particularly popular with our readers. They really are "back by popular demand." These are the other titles to look out for this month.

THE BRIDE OF THE DELTA QUEEN
by Janet Dailey

When Miss Julia Barkley, whom she had only just met, asked Selena to accompany her on a trip down the Mississippi, for moral support, Selena was happy to agree – until Miss Barkley's nephew Chance turned up on the boat. For after her first, disastrous encounter with Chance, the last thing Selena wanted was to be anywhere in his vicinity!

SONG OF THE WAVES
by Anne Hampson

With only three months to live, Wendy knew that if love did come to her she must have the strength to reject it. A luxury liner on a world cruise provided the background for her meeting with the handsome Garth Rivers . . . and she found herself in the very situation she wished so desperately to avoid.

NIGHT OF LOVE
by Roberta Leigh

The rich young Greek Leon Panos wanted to marry Alex, but she didn't feel strongly enough about him to accept his proposal – but Leon's tyrannical cousin Nicolas didn't know that, and he set firmly about breaking up the romance. All of which was to lead Alex into far deeper waters with Nicolas than either of them had foreseen . . .

Mills & Boon
the rose of romance

Doctor Nurse Romances

Romance in the wide world of medicine

Amongst the intense emotional pressures of modern medical life, doctors and nurses often find romance. Read about their lives and loves in the four fascinating Doctor Nurse romances, available this month.

NURSE WESTON'S NEW JOB
Clare Lavenham

CANDLES FOR THE SURGEON
Helen Upshall

THE RELUCTANT ANGEL
Sarah Franklin

NURSE ON NEURO
Ann Jennings

Mills & Boon
the rose of romance

Mills & Boon

Accept 4
Best Selling Romances
Absolutely
FREE

Enjoy the very best of love, romance and intrigue brought to you by Mills & Boon. Every month Mills & Boon very carefully select 4 Romances that have been particularly popular in the past and re-issue them for the benefit of readers who may have missed them first time round. Become a subscriber and you can receive all 4 superb novels every month, and your personal membership card will entitle you to a whole range of special benefits too: a free monthly newsletter, packed with exclusive book offers, recipes, competitions and your guide to the stars, plus there are other bargain offers and big cash savings.

**AND an Introductory FREE GIFT for YOU.
Turn over the page for details.**